**"We're standing under the mistletoe," he said softly, a hint of laughter in his tone.**

Tarah's gaze moved from his face upward to where he pointed. A ball of mistletoe, brightly trimmed with evergreens and a red velvet ribbon dangled precariously above them. She turned her gaze back to his, staring into his dark eyes. "Christmas is officially over."

He shrugged his broad shoulders. "It still counts. At least until New Year's."

"Says who?"

"It's an old family tradition. If you stand under the mistletoe, you can't refuse to be kissed."

"We don't have that tradition in my family."

"You're in Stallion territory. In this house those are the rules."

"Says who?"

"Says every man named Stallion in this family. Just ask them if you don't believe me."

Tarah crossed her arms over her chest, her stance widening as she faced him full on. It was a standoff of magnanimous proportions as they stared intensely at each other. Nicholas was actually taken aback when Tarah suddenly moved against him, pressing both her hands against his chest. The heat between them rose like a firestorm intent on vengeance.

Dear Reader,

I am so excited about Tarah Boudreaux and Nicholas Stallion's story that I could just bust! Pairing a Stallion with a Boudreaux came naturally once I discovered the Utah branch of the Stallion family tree. This connection felt all kinds of right!

*A Stallion's Touch* is all about love. Love overcoming obstacles. Love unexpected. Love manifested from the deepest friendship. Tarah and Nicholas's story is love in all its exquisite glory!

Family and faith are the cornerstone of all my Stallion-Boudreaux stories, and this one is no different. Faith and trust in a higher power are the reasons Tarah and Nicholas are able to transcend doubt and fears and overcome their trials and tribulations. Together they are fire and fire, and it doesn't get any better than that.

Thank you so much for your continued support. I am humbled by all the love you keep showing me, my characters and our stories. I know that none of this would be possible without you.

Until next time, please take care and may God's blessings be with you always.

With much love,

*Deborah Fletcher Mello*

www.DeborahMello.blogspot.com

# A Stallion's TOUCH

# DEBORAH FLETCHER MELLO

**H** HARLEQUIN® KIMANI™ ROMANCE

To Deborah's Diamonds—each of you is a true gem.
I greatly appreciate and love you all.

Recycling programs
for this product may
not exist in your area.

ISBN-13: 978-0-373-86469-0

A Stallion's Touch

Copyright © 2016 by Deborah Fletcher Mello

For questions and comments about the quality of this book please contact us at CustomerService@Harlequin.com.

**HARLEQUIN**®

**Printed in U.S.A.**

www.Harlequin.com

**Deborah Fletcher Mello** has been writing since forever and can't imagine herself doing anything else. Her first romance novel, *Take Me to Heart,* earned her a 2004 Romance Slam Jam nomination for Best New Author. In 2005 she received Book of the Year and Favorite Heroine nominations for her novel *The Right Side of Love,* and in 2009 she won an RT Reviewers' Choice Best Book Award for her ninth novel, *Tame a Wild Stallion.* With each new book Deborah continues to create unique storylines and memorable characters.

### Books by Deborah Fletcher Mello

### Harlequin Kimani Romance

*Seduced by a Stallion*
*Forever a Stallion*
*Passionate Premiere*
*Truly Yours*
*Hearts Afire*
*Twelve Days of Pleasure*
*My Stallion Heart*
*Stallion Magic*
*Tuscan Heat*
*A Stallion's Touch*

Visit the Author Profile page at
Harlequin.com for more titles.

# THE STALLION FAMILY TREE

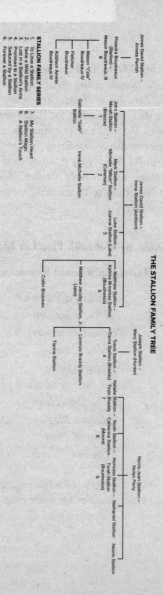

James David Stallion –
Amela Parrish

Phaedra Boudreaux
(Stallion) –
Mason Boudreaux, III
6

Mason "Cole"
Boudreaux IV

Fletcher
Boudreaux

Addison Amela
Boudreaux IV

James David Stallion –
Irene Stallion (Addison)

John Stallion –
Marsh Stallion
(Briscoe)
1

Gabrielle "Gabi"
Stallion

Mark Stallion –
Michelle "Mitch" Stallion
(Coleman)
2

Irene Michelle Stallion

Luke Stallion –
Joanne Stallion (Luke)
3

Matthew Stallion –
Katrina Broomes Stallion
(Boudreaux)
5

Matthew Jacoby Stallion, Jr. –
Lorenzo Brady Stallion
(Jake)

Collin Broomes

Tianna Stallion

Joseph Stallion –
Mary Stallion (Hunter)

Travis Stallion –
Tierra Stallion (Brady)
4

Tianna Stallion

Natalie Stallion –
Trajin Brady
7

Noah Stallion –
Catherine Stallion
(Moore)
8

Norris-Jean Stallion –
Nolan Perry

Nicholas Stallion –
Tarah Stallion
(Boudreaux)
9

Nathaniel Stallion

Naomi Stallion

**STALLION FAMILY SERIES**

1. To Love a Stallion
2. Tame a Wild Stallion
3. Lost in a Stallion's Arms
4. Promises to a Stallion
5. Seduced by a Stallion
6. Forever a Stallion
7. My Stallion Heart
8. Stallion Magic
9. A Stallion's Touch

# *Prologue*

Injection Bar was congested, overrun with medical students from Tulane University School of Medicine. The staff was working harder than normal to keep up. Tarah Boudreaux hated to add to the confusion but lifted her hand for the bartender's attention. He was tall and blond with strong Nordic features and long windblown locks, and his denim jeans and bright white T-shirt fit like a glove. He tossed her a responsive nod and gestured with his index finger. Tarah gave him a bright smile and turned her attention back to the makeshift stage.

It was the third Friday in March, Match Day. The day when graduating medical students nationwide discovered the hospital residency programs they'd been paired with to complete their graduate medical training. Tarah had interviewed with five medical facilities across the United States and although she had narrowed the list down to her top two favorites, she would gladly have gone wherever the wind blew her.

She and her fellow classmates were following a time-honored tradition, announcing the hospitals they'd been matched with over the bar's sound system. She clapped as another student with fire-engine-red hair and a lumberjack beard jumped excitedly when they called his name and waved him to the front.

"One Corona with a wedge of lime!" the bartender suddenly said, shouting over the noise into her ear.

Tarah jumped slightly, her smile still bright as she took the beer bottle from his hand. "Thanks, Milton! Put it on my brother's tab, please?"

Milton laughed. "Kendrick said he's not covering your bill any more, Tarah! You know that."

Tarah rolled her eyes. "Today's special! It'll be okay! I promise!"

Milton shook his head. "I swear, girl, you are going to get me fired one day."

Tarah giggled. "Thank you, Milton!" She gave him a wink of her eye, her lengthy lashes batting teasingly.

He nodded. "Congratulations! And tell your folks I said hello."

Turning herself back around, Tarah settled into the nervous energy that filled the room. It had taken her nine years to get to this point. Four years of college and five years of medical school—including the two semesters that she'd had to repeat for partying too much—were culminating in this moment.

The Dean of Student Affairs suddenly called her name, waving a white envelope in his hand. Her classmates all cheered, and Tarah felt her knees begin to shake. She chugged back what remained of her bottled brew, then slid off the bar stool and sauntered to the microphone.

Every eye in the room was on her, and she could feel her hand shaking as the dean slid the envelope onto her palm. She took a deep breath and then a second as she slid her thumb beneath the sealed flap and pulled the typed letter from inside. Someone in the back suddenly called her name.

"Get it, Tarah!" And the whole room erupted with a uniform cheer.

She grinned as she quickly read the letter's contents, and then her smile widened considerably. "Phoenix Hope Surgical Center!" she screamed, jumping up and down excitedly. "I'm going to Arizona!"

The room cheered with her as she rushed back to her seat to hug her friends. As the next person's name was called, Tarah was still squealing with joy. She'd been matched with her first choice, and she couldn't have been happier.

Katherine Boudreaux hugged her tightly, and Tarah melted into her mother's warm embrace. "We are so proud of you, Tarah!" the matriarch exclaimed.

Tarah's father, Mason "Senior" Boudreaux, echoed

the sentiment. "My baby girl is going to be a surgeon! Hot damn!" he proclaimed as he wiped a tear
from his eye.

Tarah was still grinning brightly. "I'm going to
Phoenix! It's the best surgical center and teaching
hospital in the nation. And I'll be training with Dr.
Harper! He's the neurosurgeon of neurosurgeons!"
she said, referring to her medical mentor, whose visit
to Tulane had inspired Tarah to consider Phoenix
Hope in the first place.

Her mother gave her one last squeeze before letting her go. "We need to call the rest of the family
to let them know your good news."

"We could just wait until they come for gradua-
tion," Tarah said, shrugging her shoulders slightly.
"Or maybe just send a group text?"

The matriarch tossed her daughter a look. "Nonsense. This is good news. We need to let them all
know, personally! Besides, it gives me a reason to
call and check on everyone," Katherine said as she
took the telephone receiver into her hand and began
to dial.

Tarah turned her attention to her father. "And I
can stay at the house in Phoenix, right? That way
I won't need to find an apartment or worry about
rent!"

Her father eyed her with a raised brow. The house
in Phoenix that she was referring to was the Paradise
Valley estate that was actually owned by her oldest
brother, Mason Boudreaux III. Mason had bought
the property a few short months after Hurricane Ka-

trina when their family had been displaced from their Louisiana home. They'd all lived in Arizona for two years while their Broadway Street property and the city of New Orleans had been rebuilt. Leaving Phoenix had been bittersweet, but Louisiana would forever be *home* as far as her family was concerned.

Senior lifted his gaze back to her eager stare. "I don't know about all that. Now that the real estate market has finally started to come back around, your brother has been thinking about selling that house. He and Phaedra like living in Dallas. I don't see them going back there, and we definitely won't be moving back to Arizona any time soon."

"I'll ask him. Mason will let me stay."

"That house is too big for you to be living in by yourself," Katherine noted, her hand cupped over the receiver of the telephone. "We'll find you a nice studio near the hospital."

Tarah shifted her gaze skyward. "I'm sure I can find a roommate or two or three."

Senior's gaze narrowed. "Now, that's never going to happen. You and your doctor friends will not be tearing up that house like it's a party palace."

Katherine interjected, "I know that idea didn't just come out of her mouth!"

"Can we at least discuss it?" Tarah shifted her gaze from one parent to the other.

Both answered at the same time, "NO!"

Tarah blew a heavy sigh past her lips. "I'm going to bed, then," she said as she turned and headed toward the door. "But I'm still calling Mason tomorrow to ask," she said.

"The answer is still no!" Senior called after her.

Behind her, Tarah could hear her mother's laughter. "That's your child. You're the reason she's so spoiled," Katherine said.

"Leave my baby girl alone! That child is just perfect!" her father countered.

Upstairs in her bedroom, Tarah pinched herself, still in awe of how sweetly things had played out. She'd been accepted into the best teaching hospital in the nation. Phoenix Hope's surgical program was in a league of its own, and the prospect of completing her medical training there was a dream come true. And to think, they'd chosen her from the thousands of applicants who'd wanted this opportunity just as much as she had. Tears welled hot behind her lids as the magnitude of that fact settled over her.

Sometimes perceived as spoiled and overindulged, Tarah, with her carefree spirit, didn't often reflect on how seriously she'd taken her medical training. Tarah had wanted to be a doctor since she was six years old and her favorite pediatrician mended her broken arm with a pink cast and a cherry lollipop. Deciding to pursue a surgical vocation had come after a strenuous medical rotation that involved a heart transplant for an aspiring cellist. With the young man's future renewed on the celebration of his eighteenth birthday, the knowledge that she'd had a part in it made the decision the easiest of her career. From that moment forward, Tarah had buckled down. Her studies were all that mattered.

After a quick shower, she pulled her shoulder-length curls into a tight bun and tied a silk scarf around her head. As she set her alarm clock, she swiped a hand across her face, wiping away the one tear that had finally fallen over her cheek. Minutes later, when her mother peeked in to check on her, Tarah was kneeling at the side of her bed, saying a prayer of gratitude toward the sky.

# Chapter 1

Stallion Ranch, the former Briscoe family property, was well over eight hundred acres of working cattle farm, an equestrian center and an entertainment complex that specialized in corporate and private client services.

Edward Briscoe, the ranch's original owner, had been one of the original black cowboys. Not long after the birth of his three daughters, Eden and the twins, Marla and Marah, he and his first wife had chosen to expand their Texas longhorn operation. They had added two twenty-thousand-square-feet event barns and a country bed-and-breakfast.

After Marah Briscoe's marriage to business tycoon John Stallion, Edward had gifted the property to them. His daughter's love for that Stallion had ended the corporate conflict that had brought the couple together in the first place. Under the Stallion family umbrella, the Briscoe property had grown steadily and was now a point of consideration for a number of government programs to assist children and families in need. But the ranch was also home to the Stallions, and the expansive property was truly a sight to behold. Even more so with the wealth of Christmas decor that lined the drive and decorated the extraordinary house.

As Nicholas Stallion pulled his brand-new Jaguar F-Type convertible into the circular driveway, joining the line of luxury vehicles parked in front of the home, he was duly impressed. Although it wasn't his first time visiting his cousin's home, each time was just as enthralling as that first. Coming together to spend time with his family made for a textbook feel-good moment, and Nicholas found himself excited to see what this year's holiday celebration would bring.

Nicholas had met his Texas cousins as an adult, the two limbs of their family tree discovering each other after the sudden death of his mother, Norris Jean Stallion. Norris Jean had been estranged from her family, leaving behind her parents and two younger brothers to follow a man who took her for granted. Nicholas and his siblings had grown up in Utah, never knowing the family left behind in Texas. Some claimed it was Stallion magic that had reconnected them, and now the two branches of the Stallion tree and their extended Boudreaux family in-laws were as thick as thieves.

His cousin John, and John's wife Marah, met him at the home's front door, wrapping him in a warm embrace.

"Yo, Nicholas! How was the drive?" John asked, the two men bumping shoulders in a one-armed embrace.

Marah kissed his cheek. "Merry Christmas! It's so good to see you again!"

Nicholas returned the greetings. "The drive was great! Santa brought me an early present, and she's some sort of sweet," he said as he gestured over his shoulder toward his new car.

"Very nice!" John exclaimed, shaking his head as he eyed the vehicle from the front porch.

A familiar voice sounded from the other side of the foyer. "You would have been here sooner if you'd caught a plane with the rest of us," Nicholas's twin brother, Dr. Nathaniel Stallion, exclaimed.

The twins both chuckled as they greeted each other warmly. "Am I the last one here?" Nicholas questioned.

"No, we're still waiting for Tarah."

A moment of confusion washed over the man's face. "Who's Tarah?"

"That would be my baby sister," Mason Boudreaux interjected, suddenly joining the conversation. Mason was married to Nicholas's cousin Phaedra, the only girl in the Dallas branch of the Stallion clan. "I didn't realize a few of you still hadn't met her until my mother pointed it out at breakfast this morning."

"That's what a medical residency program will

do to you," Nathaniel interjected. "I remember those days and the family events I missed."

Mason extended his hand toward Nicholas. "It's good to see you again, Mr. MVP!"

Nicholas nodded, a wide grin across his face. "You caught that, huh?"

"Who didn't? That was a bold statement to make," the other man exclaimed, referring to Nicholas's most recent postgame interview about his prospective championship intentions.

"More like arrogant," Nathaniel interjected.

Nicholas laughed as he shook his head. "Smoke and mirrors, bro! You have to give the fans a good show. Besides, I might as well claim the title if I aspire to it, right?"

His twin snorted, his eyes darting skyward.

Noise and laughter vibrated through the home's interior. Marah waved the men aside. "You all need to let Nicholas get a seat before you inundate us with football talk." She stole a quick glance at her wristwatch. "And it's almost time for Santa's helpers to start putting stuff together. We've got two Barbie dollhouses, some racetrack thing and at least six tricycles!"

John laughed. "I think we'll probably have more fun with the football!"

Marah narrowed her gaze at him. She stood on tiptoe to kiss his lips, gently pressing her mouth to his. "I like football, too, but not all the time, and not when there are a million things that have to be done to pull off this holiday."

John laughed as he gave her a light squeeze. "I've got you, baby! Don't you worry about anything. I personally guarantee all your elves and Santa's helpers will get everything on your list done before the chubby guy falls down that chimney!"

"Nicholas, are you hungry? There's a ton of food," Marah said, shifting the conversation.

"I could eat."

"He never stops eating," Nathaniel added. "We probably should have warned you!"

Marah laughed. "Naomi did," she said, referring to their older sister.

A hurricane of noise and limbs suddenly burst through the space, a cavalcade of youngsters racing past the adults. They ranged in age from three to almost twelve and sounded like a hurricane in the making.

"Gabrielle! Irene! Stop running!" Marah admonished. "And I mean it! You two are keeping all your cousins stirred up! Santa's not coming if you two don't get it together! How many times do I have to tell you both to set the example for the younger kids?"

Both little girls suddenly came to an abrupt halt, the others falling in line behind them. They eyed Nicholas warily. The younger of the two, Gabrielle Stallion shifted her gaze from his face to the bright white running shoes he wore on his feet. Her eyes moved from him to Nathaniel, shifting as she took in their identical features. She pointed an index finger. "You two are twins!"

The adults laughed.

"That's right," Nathaniel said. "This is my twin brother."

"Gabi, you don't remember your cousin Nicholas?" John asked, his gaze on his daughter's face.

Gabi shrugged, the gesture dismissive.

"Did you bring presents? Everyone else brought presents," Irene Stallion questioned, her small hands resting on her lean hips.

Nicholas laughed. "I did bring presents. They're still in my car. Are you going to help me carry them in?"

Irene narrowed her gaze on the man's face. "I'll go get Collin. He does things like that," she said with a shrug.

Gabi echoed the sentiment. "Collin does 'dem things. He's a big boy," she said.

"Girls can do boy things, too," Irene said matter-of-factly.

Two of the older boys looked from the girls to the adults. One small voice suddenly spoke up. "Uncle John, are we still going outside to play kick ball?"

John turned his gaze to eye the nine-year-old and ten-year-old staring at him. "We're ready when you are, Jake. But I thought you and Lorenzo were having fun playing with the girls?"

The youngster named Lorenzo gave them all an exaggerated eye roll. "Irene and Gabi are too bossy," he said emphatically.

"Am not!" Gabi snarled.

Irene snapped her head in the young boy's direction, her eyes narrowing into thin slits. "Humph!" she grunted.

Lorenzo's eyes widened, and he took a step backward, bumping into his cousin Jake.

"I'm playing, too, and I'm going to be the pitcher," Irene said as she turned on the toes of her cowboy boots. She then tossed her ponytail over her shoulder and moved toward the back of the house.

Gabi gave the boys a *take that* look as she skipped after her older cousin. The line of noise followed behind the two, the wealth of it rushing toward the other side of the home.

John called after them, "Gabi! Your mother said to stop running!"

Marah tossed up her hands. "You guys know your way to the kitchen. I need to corral the toddler brigade back upstairs to the playroom."

"I'm still trying to figure out how they all got out!" John exclaimed, his own head shaking.

He and Marah exchanged a look both answering at the same time. "Frick and Frack!" they exclaimed, referring to Gabi and Irene.

Nicholas laughed. "And how old are the girls now?" he asked.

"Gabi is eight and Irene just turned eleven." Marah answered.

"Eleven going on thirty," Mark Stallion, John's brother, suddenly interjected, hearing his daughter's name. "It's good to see you, cousin," he said as he moved to Nicholas's side to shake his hand.

Marah gave her husband a quick nod. "John Stallion, you have only two hours until all the children need to be in bed. Please tire them out before we all go crazy!" she admonished as she rushed in the direction of the noise, an argument ensuing in the other room between the younger kids.

John laughed. "You are just in time, Nicholas. How are you at running the bases?"

"I've never had any problems before," Nicholas answered, chuckling deeply.

The others all laughed with him.

"Well, Mark's daughter is one tough cookie," John interjected. "And she throws a mean ball. You may have just met your match."

The men from the Stallion and Boudreaux families and their children were divided into two teams. John was captain of one, and Nicholas had volunteered to lead the other. The women watched from the rear patio as the men and children played kick ball in the makeshift field.

Irene's mother and Mark's wife, Michelle "Mitch" Stallion, shook her head. She and Marah exchanged a look, their two daughters bickering at each other in the outfield. Despite admonishments from both their fathers, neither little girl was interested in playing nice.

"She's trying to break me," Marah said. "Gabi has made it her mission to try my last nerve and break me down."

Marah's twin sister, Marla, laughed. "It was that

parent curse. Daddy had wished that you'd have a daughter just like yourself, and voilà!"

Marah cut an eye in her twin sister's direction. "I was never that bad!"

"You really were *that* bad," their older sister Eden said.

Katherine Boudreaux chuckled. "We all have one that challenges us. Thankfully they grow out of it," she said.

"Which one of us was yours, Mama?" Maitlyn Boudreaux-Sayed asked, shifting her newborn son against her shoulder.

Her sister, Katrina Boudreaux Stallion, echoed the question. "Yeah, Mama? Which one?"

Their mother tossed them both a look. "Do you two really have to ask?"

A warm voice echoed from inside the patio door. "I'll take that as a compliment!" Tarah Boudreaux exclaimed as she rushed out to hug her family.

"Tarah!" The women called out excitedly, everyone rising to embrace her.

"You finally made it," her sister Katrina said, moving to give her a hug. "Why didn't you call? Someone could have picked you up."

Tarah shrugged. "Someone did. There was a car service waiting for me when I landed."

The women all looked at each other. Maitlyn, who was usually their go-to girl for anything that needed to be done, said, "It wasn't me this time!"

"Well, I don't care who did it. I'm just glad they did," Tarah said. Reaching for Maitlyn's baby, Tarah pulled the infant into her arms. It was her first time seeing her new nephew in person. "Maitlyn, he's beautiful!" she exclaimed, kissing the little boy's cherub cheeks. "And he's so chubby!" She looked around for the infant's older sister. "Where's Rose-Lynne?" she asked. The little girl was nowhere in sight.

Maitlyn dropped back into her seat. "Upstairs in the playroom with the nanny!" She blew out a sigh. "I love coming here. I can actually take a break! Zayn isn't an easy baby like his sister was."

"Ain't that the truth," Tierra Stallion exclaimed. Tarah imagined she was thinking about her own children, Lorenzo and his little sister Tianna. Visiting the ranch had to have been a welcome reprieve for her and her husband Travis. The distraction of cousins for their children to play with and the added care from family and trusted staff were just the beginning of the many perks afforded to them.

"I don't know about all that," Phaedra Stallion-Boudreaux offered. She rubbed a small hand against the beginnings of a baby bump. "Every time I take a break here, Mason and I get pregnant." It was her third pregnancy in as many years. Her two sons and the daughter they hoped for had begun to look like stair steps.

"I think it must be something in the water," Phaedra's sister-in-law, Dahlia Boudreaux, echoed as she waddled to her seat. It was her third pregnancy as well, the second set of twins coming to her and her husband Guy.

Katrina Stallion laughed. "At least every time you visit and get pregnant, you go home and win another film award! So there are perks!" she said as she gave Dahlia a high five.

"It's the water!" all the women exclaimed, their laughter abundant.

Katherine laughed with them. "Girls, it sounds like your problem is that you're having too good of a time during those breaks! And that don't have anything at all to do with water unless y'all are doing it in that swimming pool!"

The women all laughed again.

Tarah passed her nephew back to his mother. "So what good family gossip have I missed?" she asked, her eyes briefly shifting out to the activity on the game field.

Marah laughed. "Where do you want us to start?"

Tarah's gaze suddenly came to an abrupt halt. "Please start by telling me that tall and good-looking man out there is a family friend and not related to me by blood." Rising from her seat, she walked to the edge of the patio, and all the women turned to where she stared.

Her mother laughed, the matriarch shaking her head. "He's related to you. I'm sure of it."

Tarah's sister Maitlyn giggled. "Not really, and definitely not by blood. That's Nicholas Stallion. He's one of the Utah cousins. He's Nathaniel's twin brother. Nathaniel is a doctor, too."

Tarah grinned. "That makes him a Boudreaux

family *friend*," she said as she bit down on her bottom lip.

Out on the field, Nicholas stood with Irene, whispering something in the little girl's ear. Her smile was canyon-wide as she nodded her head at whatever he was saying. Tarah found herself surprised that he'd caught her attention. His athletic build and cocky swagger were the opposite of what she was usually attracted to. But the man was tall and buff, his build a strong, solid mass of rock-hard muscle. He moved with a hint of arrogance in his step. He was a beautiful specimen of male prowess, and Tarah imagined that there wasn't a woman who wouldn't be impressed.

"So, what does the twin who's not a doctor do?" she asked, turning her attention away from the man for a moment.

"You mean you really don't recognize him?" one of the women asked.

Tarah shook her head.

"That will just burst his bubble," someone else interjected.

Marah laughed. "Nicholas is a professional football player. He's the quarterback for the Los Angeles Marauders."

"The *star* quarterback!" one of the other women gushed.

Tarah laughed. "His feelings are really going to be hurt, then, because I *hate* football!"

Across the way, Nathaniel's eyes suddenly shifted in her direction. His gaze widened with interest, his

mouth dropping open slightly. Distracted, he missed
the ball tossed his way, the rubber sphere rolling
toward the outfield, the little girls racing after it.
The gesture was abrupt, and obvious, as everyone
turned to stare where he stared. And then he suddenly dropped to his knees, Irene slamming the rubber ball harshly into his midsection.

The Stallions and the Boudreaux were a family of
beautiful people, kindhearted, generous and loyal to
a fault. Their list of personal accomplishments was
lengthy. Between them all, they'd amassed enough
wealth to run a large country, but they were humble
and grounded in their love for God and each other.
Whenever they came together, laughter was abundant, tears were joyous and the memories were rich.
This time was no different.

Nicholas stood toward the back of the oversize
family room, his hands folded together behind his
back. Looking about the space, he was enamored
with the energy that overflowed throughout the home
and the abundance of love that embraced them. It felt
like a cashmere sweater wrapped tightly around his
shoulders. He was in awe of how life had changed
for them all since they'd found each other.

The family stood together as Reverend Milo Ber-
nard, the pastor of John and Marah's church, blessed
them. The reverend anointed the holiday season with
prayers for continued prosperity and health, giving
benedictions to send them into the new year. With
the last gesture of thanksgiving, Marah announced

that it was bedtime for everyone under the age of twenty-one. But it was only when Senior Boudreaux raised his voice that each of the kids went racing to their beds to wait for the arrival of Santa Claus. With a collective sigh, the adults all dropped into the moment, savoring the first ounce of quiet since the day had begun.

As Nicholas's gaze skated around the room, he suddenly locked eyes with Tarah, catching the young woman staring at him intently. They had officially met over dinner and then the teasing had begun, both families poking fun at the two of them. It was even more humorous when little Irene, not at all amused, declared him her boyfriend and Tarah her sworn enemy. In cahoots with her best buddy, Gabi, the girls had made it their mission to keep the two of them apart. Everyone had found it amusing, and even he'd laughed it off. But there was something about the beautiful woman that had him feeling giddy and completely intrigued.

Tarah Boudreaux's youthful exuberance was a welcome change from the women he usually encountered. Most of the females who sought out his attention wore an air of desperation like a beloved perfume. But there was nothing desperate about Tarah. In fact, she'd been aloof and dismissive, barely batting an eyelash's worth of attention in his direction.

Across the room, she was now giving him a look that had him twisting nervously in his seat, and he found himself grinning foolishly. She rose from her own chair and moved to his side, dropping down on the settee where he rested.

He took in a swift breath of air, filling his lungs to calm the nerves that had risen unexpectedly. "Dr. Boudreaux!"

"Mr. Stallion. Are you enjoying your Christmas Eve?"

"I am. How about you?"

"I forgot just how much I miss being around family over the holidays."

"When was your last time here?"

Tarah pondered the question for a quick minute. "Thanksgiving, last year. I think. It's been a good long while, but my schedule isn't the most accommodating."

"My brother says you're a surgeon? Is that right?"

She nodded. "My specialty is neurosurgery. It's usually a seven-year residency, and I have one more year and a half to go. I'll be doing a fellowship my last year in trauma and neurocritical care."

"That sounds…serious! You have to use a lot of big words in your profession, don't you?"

She laughed. "It's a lot of work, but it's well worth it."

"So, how can you hate football?" he asked, addressing one of her comments that had his cousins teasing him earlier.

Tarah shrugged, a smirk crossing her face. "Don't take it personally. I hate basketball and soccer, too. I do like tennis, though."

Nicholas laughed. "I hope you know that doesn't redeem you."

She gave him another smug glance, her eyes rolling. "Do I look like a woman who's worried about redemption?

Nicholas met the look she was giving him, his own eyes widening ever so slightly. Tarah Boudreaux was extraordinarily beautiful. Everything about her reminded him of summer sunshine, the blue water of a tropical paradise and ice cream—rum raisin with chocolate, to be specific. Light danced across her face, and her warm honey complexion shimmered as if she'd been dipped in flecks of gold. Her mouth had the sweetest hint of a pout to it, and when she smiled, her lips were intoxicating.

He chuckled again, the gut-deep rumble warm and endearing. "Honestly? You look like a woman I should probably be fearful of."

She laughed, rose from her seat and turned toward the kitchen and the throng of women who'd headed in that direction to get a jump on the holiday meal. She stopped abruptly, tossing him a look over her shoulder. "You need to be afraid, Mr. Stallion! Be very, very afraid!"

# Chapter 2

"Nicholas is my boyfriend!" Irene said emphatically, a hand on her hip. She held a brand-new basketball beneath her other arm as she tapped a high-top Converse against the hardwood floor.

Gabi nodded her head in agreement, her arms folded across her chest.

Michelle shook her head as Mark responded to their daughter's comment. "You can't have a boyfriend until you're fifty."

"Yes, I can! Can't I, Mommy?"

Mark eyed his daughter with a narrowed gaze before tossing her mother a look. "I can't handle this," he said, his stare shifting briefly in Nicholas's direction. He looked back at his wife as he pointed a finger. "Do something before I lock her away until she turns forty!"

Nicholas laughed, holding up both hands as if he were surrendering. Tarah sat across the table from him unable to contain her own giggles. Irene glared at her, which made the moment even funnier.

Everyone in the room erupted in a wealth of laughter.

"I would have to hurt someone!" Zakaria Sayed said, his daughter sitting in his lap. "They start way too young!"

Maitlyn rubbed her hand against her husband's back. "Poor Rose-Lynne. She doesn't have a clue what she's up against with all the men in this family."

Her brother nodded in agreement. "You got that right," Kendrick Boudreaux echoed as he high-fived his best friend. "Zak and I will put that nonsense to a stop, quick."

Katherine never looked up from the pot she was stirring. "Your children are going to do exactly what they want to do. You just need to ensure you give them a solid foundation to build on. He won't be the first boyfriend that baby's going to want to claim. Tarah had dozens by the time she was twelve. Then she turned eighteen, and we haven't seen a man worth his weight in salt since."

Tarah laughed. "That is not true!" she exclaimed, color rising to her cheeks.

"Which part?" Nicholas questioned, meeting her gaze.

She noted the smirk across his face. "I may have

had dozens by the time I was thirteen, but when I turned eighteen, I didn't waste my time with men who didn't meet the Boudreaux family standard!"

"That's debatable," her father interjected. "Y'all remember that boy with the squint eye?"

Tarah jumped to her feet. "No, they don't, and why are we suddenly focused on me? He's the problem. Chasing after youngsters!" she exclaimed, pointing a finger at Nicholas.

Nicholas laughed. "I did no such thing!"

Tarah leaned down toward Irene, meeting the little girl at eye level. "You don't want him to be your boyfriend," she said. "He's not very nice!"

Irene's eyes narrowed into thin slits. She gave Tarah a look before easing her way over to Nicholas's side. She dropped an elbow to his thigh as she rested her chin against her palm, leaning against his leg.

Nicholas laughed as he gave Irene's ponytail a light tug. The little girl grinned brightly in response. He winked an eye at Tarah.

Gabi moved to stand beside her friend. "That's why Santa didn't bring you gifts!" she proclaimed, cutting an eye at Tarah. "You're the one that's not nice! Nicholas is real nice."

Tarah shook her head as she stood up straight. "Santa brought me gifts!" she hissed between clenched teeth.

Gabi mimicked her Aunt's eye roll.

"Did I really just get schooled by a first grader?" Tarah shifted her eyes from one kid to the other.

"I'm in second grade!" Gabi snapped back.

The entire room roared, another round of laughter sweeping through the space.

Marah shook her head. "Gabi, Irene, that's enough out of you two. Head up to the playroom with your toys, please! Only grown-ups can be downstairs right now."

Irene grabbed Nicholas's hand. "Come play!"

Tarah laughed. "That's right!" she exclaimed. "Only grown-ups are allowed downstairs, Mr. Boyfriend!"

Nicholas laughed as Irene and Gabi both pulled him along. "Jealous much, Dr. Boudreaux?"

She rolled her eyes as Nicholas's sister Naomi eased to her side. "I think my brother likes you," the woman said, her voice low.

Tarah giggled. "I think I might like your brother."

Mason shook his head. "He's not your type. Besides, we all like him, too. No one wants to see you break his heart. And you're notorious for that!"

Tarah shot her brother a look. "I am not!"

Kendrick nodded. "Yes, you are! You chew guys up and spit them out like they're nothing. It's never pretty, so we definitely don't need you throwing Nicholas off his game."

"I know that's right!" Mark echoed. "I've bet too much money on him, so I need my cousin's head straight for game day."

Tarah tossed up her hands. "I am not a heartbreaker!" she exclaimed as she dropped down into the seat Nicholas had just vacated.

Her siblings all gave her a look, and then everyone chuckled, amusement wafting between them.

"Who all's going to the game?" John asked, looking around the room as he changed the subject.

"I think we should make it a family event," Nicholas's older brother, Noah Stallion, interjected. "Try to get everyone there to support him."

Tarah clapped her hands together. "Ohh! The championship game! I can't wait! I really hope I can get the time off."

Marah laughed. "I thought you hated football?"

"I do, but it's the *championship game*! Besides, football players are too cute in those uniforms. Who can hate a tight end with a *tight* end?"

Confusion washed over her mother's face. "I thought you all said that boy was a quarterback?"

Tarah found Christmas Day to be one of the best she'd ever had. She had missed the energy of having her siblings and their extended family together in the same space. The fellowship reinforced how much she loved, and had missed, her people while she was living in Phoenix.

Everyone's good mood swept from room to room. The laughter was intoxicating, and the whole family was drunk with joy. By midafternoon, all of the children had finally settled down, either napping away the morning excitement or cuddling quietly in a corner with a new toy or book.

Decadent kitchen smells wafted through the home as the final touches were being put on the holiday meal. Turkeys and hams had been pulled from the ovens, cakes and pies decorated the counters, and everyone's favorite foods were being transferred to serving dishes.

Heading down to the stables, Tarah had followed her nephew Collin, who'd been excited to ride the new horse that Santa had brought him. The college sophomore stood as tall as the other men in the family, his growing maturity reminding her of how quickly time was flying. She couldn't help but think that if she blinked, she might actually miss something. All the children were growing way too fast for comfort. She released a soft sigh as she sat perched on the top rail of the wooden fence that enclosed the pasture where the young man was putting the Appaloosa through his paces.

Collin's grin filled his face as he pulled the horse up to a stop beside her. "You really should come ride, Aunt Tarah! I can saddle one of the other horses if you want."

She reached out a hand to stroke the animal's neck and it neighed, its large head bobbing slightly as if it were echoing the young man's comment. "Not this time, Collin. But you go have fun. He really is beautiful!"

Collin nodded. "And here I was hoping they would get me a new phone for Christmas!"

"Sounds like you earned it. I hear things are going well for you at Morehouse."

Collin's chest pushed forward slightly. "It's getting harder, but I promised Mom I would make the dean's list every semester I'm there. I have to stay true to my word!"

Tarah smiled. "That's my guy! We're all so proud of you! Have you thought about what you want to do after college?"

He nodded. "I plan to get a law degree like Mom and Dad. And then I'm going into the family business. Stallion Enterprises keeps growing, so they are always going to need good lawyers!"

She nodded. "You go, boy! And if you change your mind, you can always practice medicine like your auntie!"

Collin shook his head. "Uh, no thanks! I don't like going to doctors, so I know I don't want to be one. I'm proud of you, though!"

Tarah laughed. "Go ride, kiddo! Enjoy that horse. What did you name him, by the way?"

Collin laughed. "Baby!"

As Collin pulled gently on the reins to turn Baby in the other direction, Tarah laughed with him.

"What's so funny?" Nicholas questioned, seeming to come out of nowhere.

His sudden appearance behind her was startling and she jumped, pulling one hand to her chest as she steadied herself with the other. "You just scared the crap out of me!" she snapped, clearly not amused.

He held up hand. "Sorry about that. I just saw you sitting here and thought I'd come say hello."

Tarah took a deep breath to calm her nerves. She cut an eye in his direction as he climbed atop the fence to sit with her. He shifted side to side, trying to make himself comfortable atop the narrow ledge.

He met the look she was giving him and smiled.

The lift of his full lips dimpled his cheeks. "So, is there a trick to this that I'm not getting?" he asked, leaning his body forward for better balance.

She chuckled. "You need a little more cushion back there. It helps."

He nodded. "No wonder you look so comfortable."

"Excuse me?"

He grinned. "It was a compliment. I was just pointing out that you have a very nice rear view. Full...and round."

There was a moment's pause as her gaze locked with his. Her eyes narrowed substantially. "Why are you looking at my ass?"

"In all fairness, I wouldn't have looked at all if the girls hadn't pointed out that you had a big butt." He laughed. "Irene thought I needed to be aware. She also said you have a big head, big feet and teeth that look goofy." He shot her a look. "Her words, not mine!"

Tarah looked out to the horizon, then shifted her gaze back out to the pasture. "I swear those two are so lucky they're short!"

"If it makes a difference," he said smugly, "they *love* your hair." He then reached out and brushed a curly strand from her eye. The gesture surprised her, causing the air to catch in her chest as she suddenly held her breath. "And you always smell really good!"

"They said I smell good?"

"No, I threw that in," he said, grinning broadly. "Like vanilla and lavender with a hint of honey. You smell like a woman is supposed to smell. Special! I was trying to help you out."

Tarah laughed, amusement dancing over her face, but she didn't bother to reply to his comment.

"You still didn't tell me what was so funny," he said. "What were you laughing about when I came up?"

"Collin named his horse Baby."

Confusion pulled at Nicholas's expression. "And that's funny because...?"

"When his mother was pregnant with Jacoby, he really wasn't happy about getting a baby brother or sister. He only wanted a horse. Then when little Jake was born and he held him for the first time, he said the baby was okay but he still would rather have had a horse named Baby instead. It was all he would talk about for months!"

"Cute," Nicholas said, nodding his head slightly as his stare shifted to where his cousin's son and the horse were moving in perfect sync with each other.

A blanket of quiet dropped over the two, the moment suddenly awkward. Nervous energy fired hot between them, feeling like a circuit board gone awry.

Tarah allowed a good few minutes to pass before she cast a quick glance in his direction. She was surprised to find him staring at her. He chuckled softly, color tinting his cheeks at being caught.

"Sorry! I didn't mean to stare, but you're just so beautiful!"

Tarah felt herself blush, the red in her own cheeks mirroring the crimson tint across his chiseled cheekbones. "Thank you," she murmured, suddenly feeling out of sorts. She couldn't help but wonder where her caustic attitude and the one-line zingers she was infamous for had disappeared to. For whatever reason, she couldn't think of anything witty to say.

She was no stranger to men commenting on her looks. Rarely did a man take a moment to know her long enough to comment on her intelligence before he was jumping at the opportunity to tell her how attractive she was. It usually struck a nerve, but there was nothing condescending, or lecherous, in Nicholas's delivery. Surprisingly flattered, she had no words.

He shifted awkwardly, still unable to make himself comfortable against the narrow rail. Amusement danced in her eyes as she watched him, and he suddenly felt as if an explanation was necessary. "Years of getting hit on the football field keep me in pain. My back and legs just aren't working with me today. I think I need a little more than some backside cushion. I'm thinking a recliner would be ideal right about now."

"Football is a rough sport, but I understand how you feel. I'm on my feet all day, every day, so even when I get a chance to rest them, they still ache."

He smiled warmly. "All the doctors I know have massive hands that look like they should be pulling tobacco in some field somewhere. You have the most delicate hands," he said.

She laughed, wiggling her fingers out in front of her. "I have a surgeon's hands. They may be small but they're steady."

"So, you really like cutting into people's flesh?"

"I love saving people's lives, curing their illnesses and helping them achieve a better quality of life."

He nodded his head. The look he gave her was endearing. "You're something special, Tarah Boudreaux!"

"And don't you ever forget it, Nicholas Stallion!"

He laughed, continuing to ask her questions about school and the hospital and other things that meant the world to her. The rest of their conversation was warm and comfortable, an easy exchange as they became better acquainted. He explained the nuances of football, described his predilection for extremely spicy foods and shared that he secretly enjoyed watching reality television.

Nicholas suddenly jumped down from his perch, his hands brushing away the dust against the back of his khaki pants. "It really has been a pleasure talking to you, Tarah. But I think it's time I sneak back down to the house." He pointed across the yard.

Turning to where he stared, Tarah saw Irene and Gabi searching him out, the two little girls making a mad dash across the fields.

Nicholas gave her a wink, and then he tore off in the opposite direction. By the time the two youngsters reached where Tarah was sitting, he had disappeared into the rose gardens. All Tarah could do was laugh.

Saying goodbye was bittersweet. Tarah wished she had another two weeks to spend with her family, but she had to report back to work the next morning. Having time off for Christmas meant she was definitely on call for New Year's. Despite the good time she'd had, she was just as excited about getting back to the hospital.

She sighed as she dragged her suitcase to the front foyer. She turned toward the family room just as Nicholas bounded down the double staircase. His eyes widened at the sight of her.

"Oh, Tarah, hey! Are you leaving?"

Tarah nodded, a slight smile pulling at her mouth. "I am. Vacation is officially over."

He came to a stop in front of her. "I really had a good time getting to know you. I hope you'll stay in touch."

Tarah laughed. "I guess that means you want me to call you."

A smirk crossed Nicholas's face. "Or I could call you?"

"You could." She reached into the backpack thrown over her shoulder, searching until she found a black ink pen. She reached for his hand, pulling it toward her. She met his bemused stare as she wrote her name and number into his palm. She then closed the cap on her pen, dropped it back into her bag and continued toward the family room, Nicholas following closely on her heels. Just as she reached the doorway, he called her name and grabbed her arm. Although there was nothing aggressive about the gesture, it clearly showed his determination.

Tarah bristled slightly. "Excuse you?" Her eyes

darted from his fingers clasped around her forearm to his face and back to his fingers.

He snatched his hand away as if he'd burned it. "I'm sorry. I just wanted to say…well…" His eyes skated about erratically as he tried to find the words to voice the thoughts suddenly racing through his head.

Tarah shifted her weight from one hip to the other, resting one hand against the curve of her waist. She eyed him with a raised brow, her look questioning.

Nicholas suddenly pointed his index finger toward the door header above their heads. "We're standing under the mistletoe," he said softly, a hint of laughter in his tone.

Tarah's gaze moved from his face upward to where he pointed. A ball of mistletoe, brightly trimmed with evergreens and a red velvet ribbon, dangled above them. She turned her gaze back to his, staring into his dark eyes. "Christmas is officially over."

He shrugged his broad shoulders. "It still counts. At least until New Year's."

"Says who?"

"It's an old family tradition. If you stand under the mistletoe, you can't refuse to be kissed."

"We don't have that tradition in my family."

"You're in Stallion territory. In this house those are the rules."

"Says who?"

"Says every man named Stallion in this family. Just ask them if you don't believe me."

Tarah crossed her arms over her chest, her stance widening as she faced him full-on. It was a standoff of gigantic proportions as they stared intensely at each other. Nicholas was actually taken aback when Tarah suddenly moved against him, pressing both her hands against his chest. The heat between them rose like a firestorm intent on vengeance. Nicholas licked his lips, the gesture ever so slight. She tilted her face upward, her eyes dancing a perfect two-step with his. There was an air of excitement that wafted between them, and just as he lowered his face to hers, his lips quivering with anticipation, she turned her head abruptly. His lips grazed the round of her cheek instead. She pushed him abruptly from her and tapped a heavy hand against his chest.

"I can just imagine the women you're accustomed to dealing with, Mr. Stallion, but I'm not that kind of girl! So please, don't get it twisted. You don't know me well enough for you to be putting your lips on mine. And that's a Boudreaux family rule! If you don't believe me, you can just ask my daddy!"

Nicholas laughed, amusement washing over his expression.

There was suddenly a wealth of applause from across the room. The two turned abruptly, surprised by the unexpected attention. They met a host of gazes, both their families clapping enthusiastically after witnessing the exchange between them.

Tarah tossed Nicholas a look, her eyes narrowing as they both blushed profusely.

Gabi's small voice suddenly bellowed across the room, her tone piercing. "Irene! Why is your boyfriend kissing that girl?"

# Chapter 3

"Paging Dr. Boudreaux to Radiology. Dr. Tarah Boudreaux to Radiology!"

Tarah paused in jotting notes onto a patient's chart. She was at the tail end of a twelve-hour shift, exhausted, hungry and unable to fathom who was paging her or why.

A nurse she recognized but didn't know by name nodded in her direction, the older woman smiling warmly. "Do you want me to call down and tell them you're on your way, Doctor?"

Tarah shook her head, taking a quick peek at the pager that had also vibrated against her hip. "No, someone's anxious for my company. No point in putting it off."

The other woman nodded, extending her hand in

greeting. "Dana Harding, CRNA. I've heard great things about you. I look forward to working with you, Dr. Boudreaux."

"Thank you. I appreciate you saying so."

Tarah's pager vibrated a second time. She placed the patient chart back onto the counter. As a soft exhalation escaped her lips, a hint of annoyance furrowed her brow.

The other woman chuckled softly. "Good luck with that," she said.

Tarah laughed with her, her name sounding over the intercom yet again. "Sounds like I'll need it," she said as she headed in the direction of the building's elevators.

Minutes later she stepped into the radiology center, hurrying toward the area's nursing station. Before she could ask who and where, the nurse behind the desk pointed her toward an office door.

With a light knock, Tarah pushed her way through the entrance and into the office space. Dr. Thaddeus Harper, Chief of Neurology at Phoenix Hope Surgical Center, stood staring out the window to the parking lot below. His hands were folded together behind his back, and he appeared to be in serious thought. He was tall and lean, his physique slim with the barest hint of muscle tone. He wore an air of wealth and accomplishment like a shroud, the abundance of it swathing every aspect of his personality. It was steeped in arrogance, and out of all the doctors in the hospital, he was probably the least liked. But he was a brilliant surgeon, considered to be the top man in his field, and that, in and of itself, garnered him much respect.

He turned as Tarah entered the room, and his face lifted with glee, the creases that edged his eyes hinting at a smile. "Dr. Boudreaux! You weren't with a patient, were you?"

"I'd just finished checking Mr. Siler's vitals. He's out of ICU and doing extremely well."

The man nodded. "Dr. Forest would have joined us but he's been called into a meeting," he said, referring to the head of radiology whose office they were in.

Tarah stood at attention as the man continued, her fingers clasped together, her shoulders pulled back.

"I'm sure you've heard of the Barton twins?"

Tarah nodded, and her eyes widened. She felt her heart begin to beat a little more rapidly. There weren't many in the area's medical field who didn't know of the Barton twins. Oscar and Henry Barton had been born a year earlier at the Phoenix Women's Hospital. They were joined at the chest wall and abdomen and shared a liver and intestinal tract. Physicians around the nation had been consulted about their pending separation, and it was rumored that a well-known celebrity had volunteered to cover the family's medical costs. The proposed operation would involve specialists from pediatrics, plastic surgery, cardiovascular surgery, urology, liver transplant surgery, orthopedic surgery and neurology. It would take close to two days from start to finish. Every doctor and intern Tarah knew hoped to be a part of the team selected. Tarah nodded. "Yes, sir! I have."

"Good." He pushed a stack of medical files in her direction. "Make sure you know everything there is to know about our patients. You'll be assisting me in the operating room. We begin practice runs tomorrow morning. The operation will take place next week. I will be reassigning all of your other patients until further notice."

Tarah fought to contain her excitement, wanting to jump up and down with joy. Her eyes were wide, misting slightly. "Thank you, Dr. Harper!"

"You've earned it, Dr. Boudreaux. Your work ethic is admirable, and everyone here in the hospital has taken notice. I look forward to you being part of the team." The barest hint of a smile pulled at the man's thin lips.

Tarah's grin was a mile wide. "I won't disappoint you, sir," she said as she nestled the file folders comfortably in her arms.

He gave her a dismissive nod. As she turned to make her exit, he called her name.

"Yes, sir?"

"Are you available for dinner tomorrow night? I'd like to discuss the case in greater detail with you." He hesitated for a brief second. "If you have time?"

Tarah paused herself as she eyed the man. She finally smiled, tossing him a quick nod of her head. "I appreciate the invitation, Dr. Harper. I look forward to it," she said softly.

This time the man's smile was wide, showcasing

his picture-perfect veneers. Before he could comment further, Dr. Forest rushed through the door. He tossed them both a look, then directed his attention to her. "Dr. Boudreaux, welcome to the team!" he exclaimed.

Tarah grinned. "Thank you, sir!"

"Dr. Harper has a lot of faith in your skills, Tarah! That says a lot. The hospital is excited to have you on board."

Tarah cut an eye in Dr. Harper's direction, his face shifting back to his usual stoic expression. His gaze had narrowed, something cold and empty seeming to seep from his blue-green eyes. Despite the respect Tarah held for the man, she understood how everyone found his mechanical nature off-putting. She turned back to Dr. Forest. "I won't disappoint, sir!"

With a tilt of his head, Dr. Forest turned his attention toward his colleague, the two men falling into conversation as Tarah exited the room. When the door closed behind her she jumped up and down, sheer joy gleaming across her face. Her excitement spilled out of every pore. The nurse at the desk stood with the telephone pressed to her ear. She laughed as she gave Tarah a thumbs-up. Dancing back toward the bank of elevators, Tarah didn't know who to call first, but she was anxious to share her good news with her family.

The rest of Tarah's day could not have gone any better. By the time she found her way home, she was exhausted but so amped with adrenaline that she'd actually considered going back to the hospital to work another shift. The only thing to stop her was having to be bright-eyed at seven o'clock the next morning to start working with the surgical team on the strategy that would change the lives of the two young boys and their parents.

As she pulled into the circular driveway, a wave of loneliness swept over her. She paused for a quick moment to take in the magnificent plantings and rolling landscape of the forty-acre compound. Her brother Mason's Arizona home sat high on Mummy Mountain with panoramic views of the city and the mountains. Citrus trees lined the driveway, and a mountain waterfall could be seen cascading in the distance. It was one of the prettiest places Tarah had ever known, but living on the impressive estate by her lonesome had started to wear thin.

The first year of her internship, she'd had three roommates. Two had since married and moved out, and the third had been evicted after throwing an unauthorized party that had left her owing her brother Mason money for the damages. Afterward she'd followed her sister Maitlyn's advice and had opted to go it alone since help wasn't needed with the housing expenses. She had her family to thank for that, and although she considered her brother's generosity a blessing, she knew her parents considered it a curse of sorts that continued to keep her spoiled.

Moving into the home, she disengaged the alarm system, then sauntered into the kitchen to make a cup of hot tea. The light on the answering machine was blinking for attention, and after she'd put a kettle on to boil, she pushed the play button to listen to her messages.

"Hey, baby girl! It's Kendrick and Vanessa. You really need to answer your cell phone or at least reply to the messages. You still have a cell phone, don't you? We just wanted to say congratulations. We know you'll do great. Give us a call when you can. Love you, little sister."

"Tarah, baby, call your parents, please. Senior says he's coming in next week to check on you, and I need you to call the landscaper so he can be around when your daddy gets there. Now don't forget, Tarah! I love you, honey!"

"Um, uh, yeah, Tarah, wow! You still have a house phone! I don't know why, but I thought I was calling your cell number. Anyway, it's Nick… Nicholas Stallion. I hope you're doing well. You were on my mind, and I thought I'd give you a call to say hello. Okay…well…give me a call when you can."

"Hey, it's me again. Nick. I forgot to give you my number. It's…"

Tarah laughed out loud as Nicholas called off the ten digits to reach him. He repeated the number three times to be sure she had it. After jotting the phone number down, she deleted all the messages, then turned back to her teapot.

She hated to admit it, but she'd thought about Nicholas often since spending time with him over the Christmas holiday. Celebrating New Year's Eve alone in the hospital ICU with a patient who'd come through brain surgery had kept him in the forefront of her mind. That night she'd wondered who he'd kissed when that silver ball had dropped to signify the midnight hour. Since then, she'd been questioning why she hadn't heard a word from him.

She had considered calling him but had talked herself out of it. Men like Nicholas had a host of women chasing after them, and she wasn't interested in being part of the pack. Besides, calling him would have required reaching out to one of her siblings, or his, for his number. She didn't need any of their family in her business that way. When another two weeks had passed with no call, she'd filed him away as interesting but unavailable. And *now* here he was, calling her.

Moving toward her bedroom, she dropped down onto an oversize recliner, pulling a cotton blanket over her legs and file folders into her lap. It was about darn time she heard from him, she thought as she sipped herbal tea from an oversize mug. And as she thought about calling him back, she couldn't wait to ask him what had taken him so long.

Nicholas opened the glove box of his car and tossed in his cell phone. He took a deep breath, hesitating briefly before finally closing the compartment door. He had tried to reach Tarah four times now, and each time he'd gotten her voice mail instead. He had yet to hear her voice, and he couldn't help but wonder why she hadn't returned his calls. The silence had him feeling some kind of way. *Every* woman Nicholas had ever been interested in *always* called him back.

Twisting in his seat, he reached into the back and grabbed his gym bag. He sighed, then exited the vehicle and engaged the car alarm. As he moved from the parking garage to the entrance of the team's training facility, fans and groupies asking for his autograph and vying for his attention besieged him.

Although he appreciated their interest, his mind was elsewhere, and he breezed right past the crowd, barely bothering to nod his head or acknowledge any of them. He ignored the catcalls, and as someone snapped his photograph, he imagined the headlines that would surely ensue about his attitude.

He had become notorious for what the media called mood swings and what sports enthusiasts had labeled bad behavior. Admittedly, his responses to the stress associated with the game hadn't always been stellar, but few people truly knew him or his heart. Nicholas had learned early on that despite the boatloads of money and time he donated to the numerous organizations he supported, it was the tantrums and flagrant outbursts that kept his name in the headlines and the cameras focused on him. That, along with some seriously impressive plays on the football field, kept his name in everyone's mouth. It had become just another part of the game that he'd learned to manipulate and play well. The payoff made him an endorsement gold mine as long as he never took it so far that he was an embarrassment to the team, the league or his family.

As the gym door slammed close behind him, he hurried down the short length of hallway toward the locker rooms. Once inside, he was assaulted by the smell of sour funk. The place reeked of sweat, feet and musk, masked by too much cologne and not nearly enough soap. Nicholas grimaced. Despite the number of times he had come and gone from the space over the years, he had never grown accustomed to the smell.

His arrival was met with amused looks as the whole team turned to stare in his direction. The team's head coach stood with his arms crossed over his chest, annoyance creasing his brow. Nicholas's eyes shifted from side to side as he took a swift inhalation of air.

"You're late, Stallion!" the Marauder coach, Marcus Brandt shouted. "Again!"

Nicholas dropped his bag to the floor in front of his locker. He shrugged his broad shoulders and proffered an apology. "Sorry, Coach. It was unexpected. Something came up."

"We're going to the big game, Stallion. If you actually want to play in that game, you need to get your ass here on time!" the man ranted, spewing a lengthy list of expletives at Nicholas. "You're lucky I don't fine your ass. I just so happen to be in a good mood!"

Nicholas didn't waste the breath to respond. He wasn't moved by the profanity-laced diatribe, and he saw no reason to reply in kind. He himself didn't cuss, his older brother Noah having told them time and time again that a man who needed to punctuate his point with obscenities really didn't have a point to make. Neither he nor any of his brothers had ever felt a need to sit around with their buddies and trade vulgarities. And it wasn't often that Nicholas allowed any other man to swear at him without him putting the fool in check. Coach was an exception to that rule. Despite the exchange, he considered the coach a friend and had much respect for the man and his position. But his body language tightened and his eyes narrowed, an air of indignation rising with a vengeance.

The expression across his face spoke volumes, and the coach suddenly swallowed hard, shifting his gaze around the room to avoid looking directly at the man he was chastising. The tension was palpable, and one of the other players suddenly slammed his helmet against a metal locker.

"Let's do this!" another teammate screamed, all of them anxious to get out on the field and hit something.

After another two minutes of a pep talk, the coach dismissed the team, and they headed in the direction of the field. He sauntered slowly to Nicholas, who still stood where he'd stopped. The two eyed each other warily.

"Why do you have to bust my chops, Stallion?" Coach Brandt questioned. He stood with his hands on his hips, his eyebrows lifted in query. "You are taking us to the Big Game! The Big Game! You're one of the best damn players in the league, and you need to be setting an example for all the others. Instead, you're giving me a hard time!"

Nicholas took a deep breath and let it out slowly. He met the look Brandt was giving him with one of his own, wondering why the man felt the song and dance was necessary. Nicholas didn't always do what was expected of him, but he had never once *not* done his job and done it well. And Brandt knew that. In the years he'd played for the team, he could count on one hand the number of times he'd been late for anything and have more than half his fingers left over. To Nicholas's chagrin, Brandt often played to the cameras and the other players, needing to laud his position whenever he had an audience.

"You done?" Nicholas finally asked, clearly not impressed.

Brandt lowered his voice. "Hey, you know everyone already thinks I give you too many passes. Just this morning someone was whining about you being the coach's favorite."

"Just this morning?"

"Well, maybe not this morning, but I heard it once this week already."

Nicholas chuckled softly. "I should be your favorite. Me scoring more points and gaining more yardage in a single game is what got you to the championship. Breaking the records I've already set is what's going to win you that championship ring. I know it and so do you."

"Yeah, yeah, yeah!" The man grinned. "So, is

everything okay? Nothing we need to worry about, I hope."

Nicholas shook his head. "Everything's fine. It won't happen again. At least, not this season. I can't speak for next year, though." He turned to hang the last of his street clothes in the locker, slamming the door closed after pulling a jersey over his head.

Brandt nodded, extending his hand. The two bumped fists, and Nicholas turned in the other direction, following the other players to the football field.

## Chapter 4

Tarah had been far from comfortable when she arrived for her dinner meeting with Dr. Harper. Kai, the five-star restaurant he'd selected, was located in the Sheraton Wild Horse Pass Resort and Spa in the Gila River Indian Community near Chandler. The award-winning eatery was renowned for its Native American cuisine, and with the diamond awards earned by their executive chef, it was a member of an elite group of dining establishments. Tarah wished she'd bothered to check the reviews before she'd left the hospital. She shut down the search page on her smart phone and gloomily exited her car.

Walking up to the entrance of Kai, it was obvious she was underdressed. Unfortunately, going home to change wasn't an option since she was past the point of arriving fashionably late. The black slacks and white button-down blouse she wore didn't begin to compare to the designer wardrobes of the other women in the room. In fact, with her thick curls pulled into a high bun and no makeup adorning her fresh face, Tarah looked more like a member of the staff than a patron.

Dr. Harper had already been seated when the hostess escorted her to his table. His stare had been critical, but as he'd risen from his seat to pull out her chair, he'd remained quiet. Admiring the gray silk suit he wore with a white dress shirt and red print necktie, Tarah felt overwhelmingly out of place. Her discomfort was painted across her face like a bad makeup job.

There was a moment of comfort when he dove right into business, quizzing her on the day's training. But by the time the waiter came bearing their appetizers, her discomfort returned with a vengeance. Their conversation had taken a personal turn. He was suddenly asking questions about her relationships and the men she'd dated in the past. When the entrée was set in front of her, she knew beyond any doubt that dinner had been a monumental mistake.

Dr. Harper suddenly sat back in his seat and stared at her. "You don't date much, do you?" he asked, his tone dry and staid.

"Excuse me?"

"You look like you're headed to the grocery store," he said, his gaze sweeping over her face. "And all we've really talked about is medical procedures."

Tarah took a deep inhalation of air. "I don't date at all, Dr. Harper. I…"

"Please, call me Thaddeus," he said, interrupting.

She hesitated. "I don't date at all, sir. And I wasn't expecting…" She paused a second time, choosing her words carefully. "I wasn't expecting to be ambushed with lobster and wine when I understood this to be a business meeting over hot dogs and french fries."

Dr. Harper laughed. "Touché! I guess I should have been more specific about our dinner plans."

Tarah rested her fork on her plate and folded her hands together in her lap. "About *your* plans, sir, and yes, you should have. Asking a girl to grab a bite to eat doesn't imply the likes of this," she said, gesturing with her hands.

The two locked gazes briefly before Dr. Harper snatched his eyes from hers. His cheeks were crimson and he fumbled with the cloth napkin in his lap. "Well, I'm still glad you're here," he mumbled nervously.

"I'm not sure what you were expecting, Dr. Harper," Tarah said softly, "but I really believed we were meeting solely to discuss the Barton twins."

Dr. Harper smiled, shifting slightly in his seat. "You're a stunning woman, Tarah. I was certain you knew I was attracted to you."

She shook her head. "No. I really didn't."

"Well, now you do. I would really like for us…"

His comment was interrupted by her cell phone's ringtone. She took a deep breath, glancing down to the number flashing on the screen. "Excuse me," Tarah said. "I need to answer this." She pulled the device to her ear. "Hello?"

"Tarah, hey, it's Nicholas. How are you?" His

voice was deep and rich, a seductive baritone that resonated through the phone line.

She wanted to smile but she forced herself to keep her expression and her tone bland. "Yes, hello. How can I help you?"

Nicholas was slightly taken aback by her coolness. "I was just calling to say hello. Is this a good time to talk?"

Tarah shot Dr. Harper a quick look. She paused as if she were still listening to something Nicholas was saying on the other end.

"Oh, my!" she exclaimed, drawing a hand to her chest. "Is it serious?"

She could hear the confusion in Nicholas's voice. "Is what serious?"

She ignored him, still speaking into the receiver. "No, no, it's no problem. If I leave now I can be back at the house in thirty minutes. Just hold on. And *don't* hang up," she commanded. "I just need to let my associate know."

Meeting the look Dr. Harper was giving her, Tarah didn't bother to cup her palm over the receiver, unconcerned about Nicholas hearing anything that would be said. "I'm so sorry, but a pipe burst at my house, and my neighbor says water is pouring everywhere." She stood up. "I really hate to rush off, but I have to leave."

Dr. Harper stood with her. "Do you need me to follow you home? I might be able to help."

Tarah gave him one of her brightest smiles, her head tilting slightly. "No, I'll be fine. I appreciate the offer, though," she said as she grabbed her handbag. "Thank you for dinner. I had a very nice time. I'll see you in the morning."

Dr. Harper brushed a large hand across her shoulder. "I hope we can finish our conversation soon."

Tarah nodded. "Of course," she answered and then turned, almost running out of the restaurant.

Once outside, she moved quickly to her car and hopped inside. As she pulled out of the parking lot, she engaged the Bluetooth on her cell phone. She could hear Nicholas breathing on the other end. "How did you get this number?" she resumed their conversation as she drove into the early evening traffic.

"Are you talking to me?" Nicholas asked, the barest hint of attitude in his tone.

Tarah met his emotion with attitude of her own. "Who else would I be talking to?"

"Whoever that man was you were trying to get away from. So, who was he?"

Tarah laughed. "He wasn't anybody."

Nicholas wasn't sure what was funny, but he couldn't help but laugh with her. Her infectious tone eased every ounce of tension between them.

She shifted the conversation. "You still didn't tell me how you got my cell phone number."

"My sister Naomi called Maitlyn and asked for it."

Tarah laughed again. "Cute!"

"Why haven't you returned my calls?" he questioned.

"Why did it take you so long even to call me?"

"Is answering a question with a question something you do often, or do you reserve these one-sided conversations for select people?"

"Only very special people!"

Nicholas grinned into his receiver. "So I am special to you! That's good to know. You had me in my feelings for a minute there."

Her eyes rolled, a wry smirk pulling at her lips. "That sounds like a personal problem to me."

He laughed. "Really, who were you trying to get away from?"

"One of the doctors from the hospital. We were supposed to be having a business meeting, but he… well…it…" she trailed off. She then reflected on what had happened earlier that evening and the huge fiasco she hoped to prevent.

Her tone changed, and Nicholas felt himself bristle with concern. "He didn't do anything to you, did he?"

"No," she finally responded. "We just got our wires crossed." Not finding it necessary to rehash how she and the good doctor had gotten off track with each other, she was ready to bring the subject to a close. "It was just time for me to leave, and your call gave me a way out. I guess I need to thank you."

"Any time. In the future, just text me and I'll be glad to assist. We can have a secret code that we use with each other. Like 911 or something."

She giggled. "911? Really? That would be some secret!"

"I said or *something*! If you text me 911, I'll know you need me ASAP, and you can trust that I'll be there. But it can be whatever you want."

Tarah felt a smile appear across her face. "So, how have you been?"

"As well as can be expected, I guess. Focused on the big game coming up more than anything else."

"The Big Game! That's quite an exciting accomplishment."

"It is, but I'll be glad when it's over. Between practice, the press junkets and people pulling at me, I've about had enough."

"What? Nicholas Stallion isn't enjoying all the attention he's getting? Who are you and where did my friend go?"

Nicholas chuckled warmly. "I'm glad you consider me a friend."

"We are practically family."

"Please don't say you look at me like a big brother. I'll be crushed."

"More like a cousin."

"A kissing cousin, I hope?"

She giggled again. "You don't quit, do you, Mr. Kiss-Me-It's-Mistletoe!"

"You can't blame me for trying. I bet that guy you were with wanted to try, too."

Tarah cringed at the thought. She didn't bother to comment. A pregnant pause suddenly blossomed between them, and Tarah fell off into her own thoughts. She noticed that neither of them seemed concerned or even aware of the time that had lapsed.

"I'm glad you finally caught up with me," she suddenly said. "And I'm sorry I didn't call you back sooner."

"I'm glad, too," Nicholas responded. "I really wanted to hear your voice again."

Tarah felt a wave of warmth bubble in her midsection. For the first time since she'd left the hospital earlier that evening, she was completely at ease. Comfort settled over her shoulders like a favorite wool blanket. "Next time you need to call sooner," she said smugly.

"Next time you should call a brother back when he does call."

Tarah laughed and Nicholas laughed with her. Their conversation continued as she pulled into the driveway of her home. They talked about the family, their friends, places they hoped to travel, foods they enjoyed. Tarah shared stories about her patients, and Nicholas talked about the other players on his team. It wasn't until hours later, when she realized it was well after midnight, that she thought about saying good-night. But before they disconnected their call, she had one last question to ask.

"Nicholas?"

"Yes?"

"Whatever happened with you and that toddler you were dating? Are you two still a thing?"

Laughing heartily, Nicholas disconnected the call.

Tarah's sisters were all laughing. The conference call with Katrina, Kamaya and Maitlyn had taken place when Tarah had called to give Maitlyn a hard time about letting Nicholas have her cell phone number.

"If you had called him back, he wouldn't have had to call me."

Tarah giggled. "Weren't you the one who taught me that you needed to keep a man hanging every now and again so he'll want you more?"

Maitlyn laughed. "I didn't teach you that."

"Mama taught us that if you need to play games with a man, he's not the one for you," Katrina interjected.

"I guess that all depends on the kind of games you want to play," Tarah said jokingly.

"That's why Mama said she's never going to find a good man," Kamaya teased.

Tarah snapped. "I'm going to find a good man! In fact, I think Nicholas is a very good man."

The other three women went silent.

"What?" Tarah questioned, wishing they were all in the same room so she could see her sisters' faces. "What's wrong with Nicholas?"

"There's nothing wrong with Nicholas," Katrina said. "All of the Stallion men are good men. I married one, remember?"

"It's something in their DNA," Kamaya interjected. "They're all just too special for words! Hell, I'd marry one if I could."

The trio laughed.

"Nathaniel Stallion is still available," Tarah noted. "I don't think he's dating anyone."

"Nathaniel is *not* my type," Kamaya concluded.

Maitlyn laughed. "You have a type?"

"You know your sister likes them blond and blue-eyed!" Katrina exclaimed.

"We're not talking about how I like them," Kamaya said with a giggle. "We're talking about how your baby sister is about to toss her goodies at that football player."

"I have never tossed my goodies at any man!" Tarah said emphatically. "In fact, my goodies are fully intact and perfectly packaged, waiting for the right guy with a discerning sweet tooth."

Kamaya laughed. "And she has a bridge she'd like to sell us, too!"

"Are you still a virgin?" Katrina suddenly asked. "Because that sounds like you're still a virgin!"

"There is no way she is still a virgin," Kamaya interjected. "I know for a fact she gave it up to that boy with the squint eye. The one who had eaten the last slice of chocolate cake that Mama had saved for Senior. I know you all remember that!"

The laughter was loud and abundant as they all reflected back on that boy and their father's favorite chocolate cake. Tarah had been head over heels in lust with the star basketball player. She'd been a freshman, young and dumb and excited by the attention the lanky senior forward was paying her. For weeks he took up space in their family room, everyone tripping over him every time they turned around. His last day there, he'd cleaned out the refrigerator, consuming whatever wasn't nailed down, including the last slice of dark chocolate pumpkin cake that their mother had saved for Senior. Everyone in the house had known not to touch the sliver of sweet dessert that had been slathered in a decadent ganache. When Senior discovered it missing, he'd been livid, and the tongue lashing he had given the boy had been the punch line at many family dinners afterward.

"Tarah's maintaining a self-imposed celibacy. She has been ever since she moved to Phoenix. I thought you all knew that," Maitlyn said matter-of-factly, pulling them all back to the conversation.

"She hasn't let a man near her stuff for over six years," Kamaya added.

"Only battery-powered Bob!" Maitlyn said with a soft chuckle.

"No one told me that," Katrina said, an air of surprise in her tone. "Six years? Really, Tarah?"

They all went silent again, waiting for Tarah to say something. Instead, she stared off into the distance, her mind muddled with thought. Her decision to abstain from sex had actually been at her mother's behest. A late night conversation between them before she'd left New Orleans had caused Tarah to reevaluate some of her choices. Katherine pointed out that Tarah too often acted before she took time to think. Her mother's observation made her more mindful of how she continued to do things. Katherine adding that most of her relationships were less than stellar, with Tarah dating boys and not men, had been enough to let Tarah know that her energy would be better served not trying to have it all without the work and effort a healthy relationship required. As her mother had admonished, she could have both a career and family, but she needed to have a plan. She needed to focus. Celibacy has been the first step.

"I cannot believe the way you three sit around talking about me like I'm not even here," she finally said, pretending to be insulted. "My feelings are actually hurt."

"Yeah, yeah, yeah," Kamaya chuckled. "Cue the violins!"

They all laughed again.

"So, really," Katrina persisted, wanting all the details. "Because I swear, this is the first time I'm hearing this!"

Tarah shook her head. "Technically I'm not a virgin, but when I started my residency I made the conscious decision to refrain from sex until my wedding night. I didn't want the distractions during my surgical training, and you all know how a man can be a distraction. Just ask the judge!"

Katrina laughed. "What do you mean, just ask me?"

"She's right," Kamaya said. "If I recall correctly, you had been naked under your judicial robes one day after you and your Stallion had done it in your office during recess."

"I was not…!" Katrina started, fighting to keep her voice calm.

"Yep, you were naked," Maitlyn said.

Katrina laughed. "You were not supposed to tell that!"

"There are no secrets here," Kamaya stated. "We share everything."

"Then how come I didn't know Tarah was doing the born-again virgin thing?" Katrina asked.

"I don't know," Maitlyn said, "because even the boys know. Ask your brothers about it. Or your husband. I'd bet Matthew knows!"

"Hey, the way news spreads through this family, I'd be willing to bet that even Nicholas knows by now!" Kamaya chuckled.

"I wouldn't take that bet," Katrina said. "Because clearly I never hear anything."

"On that note," Tarah said, "I have to get back to work." She'd been sitting in her car in the hospital parking lot for the bulk of their conversation. Her thirty-minute lunch break would be over in less than five minutes.

"I need to run, too," Katrina said. "Jake has a T-ball game this afternoon, and I promised Matthew I'd meet him downtown."

"Before you go, Tarah," Maitlyn said, turning the conversation in another direction, "when do you want to fly in for the game?" Maitlyn was responsible for arranging transportation for the family to the big play-off game and Tarah was sure her to-do list was lengthy. "You are still coming, right?"

Tarah shook her head as if her sister could see her. "I'm not sure. It's all going to depend on the Barton twins!"

The masseuse hit a particularly sensitive spot behind Nicholas's right calf. He moaned loudly, the sound resonating from a place deep in the pit of his stomach.

"Damn, bro!" Nathaniel Stallion said, looking up from the documents he was reviewing.

Nicholas laughed as he lifted his head to stare in his brother's direction. "Sorry about that."

His brother laughed with him. "Has it been that long since a woman's touched you?" Nathaniel teased.

"You know that women are off-limits right now. During the season I reserve all my energy for the football field. I can't risk being off my game, and every woman I've ever met has tried to do just that."

"That's because you go through them like water, and they're trying to hold on to you like glue."

"I don't know what it is. I just know I don't have time for it."

"You take it to the extreme, though. I understand refraining from sex before game night, but there are usually two or three days prior to each game that you can...*blow*...off some steam."

The young woman kneading the tightness out of his muscles smiled down at Nicholas as she trailed the heel of her palm up and down the length of his thigh. She tossed Nathaniel a quick look and winked, and he winked back.

Nicholas shrugged, settling back into the massage table's face hole, the surrounding memory foam cushioning his head. He allowed his mind to drift, falling into the quiet of the soft music that billowed in the background. His body finally relaxed, each sinewy muscle feeling like melted butter. It was the most relaxed he'd been in weeks, and knowing it would only last a short time allowed him to savor the sensation all the more.

For a moment he lay reflecting on his brother's comment. He didn't say so out loud, but casual sexual encounters were the last thing on his mind. The mere thought of a quick few minutes with a woman whose name he barely knew made him wince. Those days were far behind him, and he couldn't remember when he had started to feel that way. Just that he was done and finished with the playboy lifestyle others assumed he relished, one that too many of his fellow teammates were trying to master. His thoughts were suddenly interrupted by his brother's voice.

"Have you spoken to Tarah? Did she ever call you back?"

Nicholas lifted his head slightly and cut an eye in his brother's direction. He found himself suddenly regretting having said anything to his twin about the beautiful woman, wishing he'd kept his musings about Tarah to himself. But she had been on his mind, and he had needed to vent. He'd found himself missing her since their Christmas encounter. He missed the banter between them. Her teasing and the overt flirtations had become a pivotal pleasure in their relationship, if you could call what they shared a relationship. He missed her smile, and her laughter made him feel good about everything.

As he lay there thinking about her, the muscles suddenly tightened across his back and neck. The faintest hint of a rising erection began to press tight between his legs. He couldn't help but be grateful that he was lying on his stomach. He tried to ignore his brother still eyeing him with a steely gaze.

Nicholas shook his head. "No, she didn't call me back," he answered before he dropped his head back down. He closed his eyes and took a deep breath. Nathaniel didn't need to know about his conversation with Tarah or the half dozen talks they'd had since. He wasn't interested in sharing the details he knew his brother would want to hear. The little white lie was a necessary evil, he reasoned.

Nathaniel shook his head. "Maybe it's for the best. Had anything happened between you two and then you did something to mess it up, it would make family gatherings awkward."

"Why would you think I'd be the one to mess things up?"

"You don't have a stellar reputation with women. I know your entire history with the opposite sex, remember?"

"You're one to talk," Nicholas said with a chuckle. "You mastered the art of one-night stands. Everything I know I learned from you."

Nathaniel shrugged, a wry grin filling his face. "I may love 'em and leave 'em, but I leave 'em *immensely* satisfied!"

The two men laughed heartily. As the masseuse exited the room, Nicholas observed her slip Nathaniel her telephone number and him the bill for services rendered.

## Chapter 5

"A bass pro? Really?" Tarah questioned. She shifted the camera screen on her computer, more of her face and less of her body showing on the video call.

Nicholas nodded his head, smiling brightly into the camera on his end. "Yep! I wanted a career in bass fishing. Noah used to take us fishing when we were little. One summer he entered all of us in a local fishing competition and I won. I thought, what a wonderful way to make money. So why not earn a living doing what I love most?"

Tarah laughed. "So how did you go from bass fishing to football?"

"I was really *good* at football. It paid for college, and then the pros came calling."

"So you gave up on your dream of bait and fried fillets?"

Nicholas laughed. "Not at all. I plan on pro fishing being my retirement career."

"Well, I've never wanted to be anything but a doctor. When I retire, I plan to open a clinic in a third world country, providing free medical care to the poor and disenfranchised."

"You sound like a world summit pamphlet!"

Tarah giggled. "I sound like my father."

Nicholas couldn't help but smile brightly as he watched her grinning back at him. She was a daddy's girl, and it was written all over her expression. "I like your father. He's very cool for an old guy!"

She nodded her head in agreement. "Don't ever say that to his face," she responded. "He hates when we refer to him as old, and it would really piss him off if he knew we all thought he was cool. His favorite saying has always been that he's our parent first and he isn't supposed to be our friend."

"I'll keep that in mind," Nicholas said.

"What about your father?" Tarah asked.

"What about him?"

"I imagine he's very proud of you. Don't all men secretly want their sons to be superstar athletes?

Nicholas shrugged his broad shoulders, the gesture moving him out of the camera angle for a brief second. "I wouldn't know. I don't know anything about the man."

"Nothing?"

"I know his name and that's about it."

"I'm sorry."

"Don't be sorry. It's not your fault the guy was no more than a sperm donor."

Tarah blew a soft sigh, noting the sudden mist in Nicholas's eyes. It didn't take a rocket scientist to figure out that the subject of his father was a sore spot for him. His entire demeanor had changed, his shoulders rolling forward, his brow line furrowing. Even his tone seemed heavy. The laughter that had just shaded his voice was gone in an instant.

She changed the subject. "Did you and your twin dress alike when you were younger?"

"Nathaniel and I *still* dress alike! It's the craziest thing. We have the same tastes, like the same designers, and will show up wearing the exact same suit not knowing the other had bought it."

Tarah laughed. "I'm sure that's a sight to behold!"

"It's made for some interesting moments!"

Their conversation continued for a good long while. It was one of many they'd had since Tarah had finally answered that first call. She had been the one to insist they start video chatting with each other. It had taken their communications to a whole other level.

Not overly computer proficient, Nicholas had been reluctant, but Tarah had talked him through setting up his Skype account and engaging in their first video call. From the second her face filled his computer screen, her bright smile showing in real time, he was hooked. He'd loaded the application on every device he owned to ensure he never missed an opportunity to make their long-distance calls feel like she was almost right there in the room.

She shifted her body again, and for a second he caught sight of lace panties and bare legs.

"What are you wearing?" he questioned, moving forward in his seat and closer to the screen.

Tarah's eyes widened. She snatched the bedspread across her backside, covering anything that might have been exposed.

Nicholas laughed. "If I'd known we were going to have that kind of conversation, I would have taken my clothes off and gotten comfortable, too!"

She laughed with him. "We are not having *that* kind of conversation!"

"We should. White lace looks really good on you."

Tarah tossed him a look. "This is the last time we video chat while I'm in bed," she said.

"Don't change up your routine on my account," he said. "I like seeing you in bed."

Tarah felt herself blush, color warming her cheeks. There was an air of innocence about her that Nicholas found refreshing. She made him smile, the wealth of it gleaming out of his dark eyes. She met the look he was giving her with one of her own, and he wished there weren't hundreds of miles and a computer sitting between them.

"I'm sorry I won't be able to make your game," Tarah suddenly said softly. "I was really hoping to be there."

Disappointment suddenly wafted across his face. "I'm going to miss you," he said. "I was really looking forward to you being there to celebrate with me, but I understand how important your work is to you."

"It is important to me, but I'll still be rooting for you."

"It's all good as long as you're not blowing me off for that doctor friend of yours."

She shook her head. "I told you, he was no one you needed to be concerned about. He and I know where we stand with each other and where we don't. And for certain, I am not interested in him."

"But is he interested in you?"

She giggled nervously. "Of course not!"

There was a hint of uncertainty in Tarah's voice and she cleared her throat, hoping Nicholas didn't pick up on it. Truth be told, she wasn't quite sure where things stood with her and the good doctor. When they'd next seen each other, he'd had nothing at all to say about their disastrous dinner date. He'd been exceptionally professional, and she'd felt as if they might be able to find balance with each other. Then he'd started with comments and innuendo that were more appropriate for lovers, or lifelong friends who knew their boundaries with each other. It had all made her uncomfortable, and when she told him so, it was like a switch had been turned off. His personality became cold and indifferent, his expressions stiff and stoic. She found him flipping from one extreme to the other, and she'd quickly become proficient at avoiding the man unless it was absolutely necessary for them to be in each other's presence. As she thought about it, she didn't feel a need to share with

Nicholas. She saw no point in making the issue bigger than it needed to be.

"I'll make sure to watch the game on TV, and I'll be shaking my pom-poms for you. I used to be a cheerleader, you know. In high school *and* college," she said, deflecting the conversation.

"Why does that *not* surprise me?" His grin was canyon-wide, showcasing a beautiful snow-white smile.

"I could shake them for you in person, *if you win*, of course. Once you're done celebrating after the game, maybe you can plan a trip to Phoenix?"

"Is that an invitation, Tarah Boudreaux? Are you asking me to come to Arizona to see you?"

Tarah paused for a fraction of a second. Nicholas watched as she suddenly rolled onto her back, the covers falling away as the length of her long legs extended upward toward the ceiling. She flexed one pedicured foot and then the other, then bent both legs downward before rolling back to her stomach. The gesture was teasing as she flashed him another peek at her bare flesh and her high-cut lace panties. Amusement danced across her face and his.

"You said once the season was over, you needed to take a break. I was just giving you a few suggestions," Tarah finally answered.

"Starting with Phoenix and ending with Phoenix?"

"Phoenix is a beautiful place to visit." The look in her eyes was both demure and coquettish.

Nicholas grinned, a hint of mischief in his own

gaze. "I can't wait for you to show me what makes
it so special!"

Their laughter continued for hours. Midnight
came and went, and the two were still discovering
things about each other. Tarah learned that Nicholas
was not a fan of fried chicken or pasta and he de-
tested mustard and ketchup, preferring mayonnaise
on his hot dogs and hamburgers. He owned a house-
boat on Lake Union in Seattle, Washington, and he
preferred the floating home to his penthouse apartment in Los Angeles. That one home, his car and
his favored Rolex watch had been his only luxury
purchases since joining the league, and despite what
some people thought, material possessions meant
very little to him.

Tarah had allowed herself to share things with
him that she'd never purposely shared with anyone. Few others knew that she loved classical music
and that she read Shakespeare for pleasure. Nicholas could only smile when he discovered she had a
sweet tooth for fruit pies and ice cream and that she
had never ever eaten popcorn. She had told him that
the puffed grain reminded her of a toadstool she'd
eaten when she'd been small that had sickened her.

They teased and taunted each other, falling into
an easy rhythm that Nicholas found comforting. Like
that first time, and each time thereafter, saying goodbye proved to be difficult at best.

"One of us needs to hang up," Nicholas said, his
quiet tone like the gentlest of caresses. "You need to
be up early, don't you?"

Tarah nodded. "So do you."

He nodded. "Will you call me tomorrow?"

"No."

He smiled. "Don't call me. I'll call you."

"Wear something sexy when you do," she said, her mouth lifting in an upward bend. "Wear lace."

Nicholas laughed. "Hey, I have no problem showing you mine if you'll show me yours!"

Tarah's laugh was the most exquisite sound. It was vibrant and airy, like the sweetest breeze on a perfect spring afternoon. When she laughed, Nicholas couldn't do anything else but laugh along with her. They had played telephone tag for most of the day, so when they finally caught up with one another, he was excited to hear her laugh. They'd been talking for over an hour.

"People always have the wrong impression about me," she said, still giggling.

"We're talking about your brothers," Nicholas said. "I would think they know you."

"They're usually wrong. Just like I'm sure you and your brothers are with Natalie."

"My sister is spoiled rotten."

"Exactly! My family says the same thing about me, but I assure you that I am not spoiled. I'm perfectly okay with not getting my way."

Nicholas chuckled. "Are you selling bridges now, too?"

"As a matter of fact, I have a pyramid deal you might be interested in!"

Nicholas shifted his body, adjusting his computer screen to follow. "Okay, so you really aren't spoiled. You're an okay cook, not great, just okay, and you should be nominated for a Nobel Peace Prize."

"I'm also very philanthropic, and despite what some people might think, I don't have a vain bone in my body. I might be a little self-absorbed, but I'm definitely not vain," she concluded, her laugh floating through their video connection.

Nicholas shook his head, amusement dancing across his face.

"But what about you?" Tarah asked, changing the subject. "I hear you're a bit of a playboy. Is that true?"

"You did not hear that about me!"

"Oh, yes I did. In fact, there was an article about it in one of those supermarket rags. Something about you having dated a lingerie model, a stripper and a reality star all in the same month. It said you get around."

He paused, pretending to be contemplating the statement. "I did date a reality star once a long, long time ago, but I don't recall a stripper."

Tarah laughed and a warm tingle rippled across his spine. "How could you not recall?"

"That's my story and I'm sticking to it. I have no recollection of ever making it rain. Ever!"

"So, you're not only a bit of a playboy but also insensitive to the women you date. You don't even remember them!"

"Not at all. I'm a very sensitive individual."

"Do you date a lot?" Tarah asked, her humor brimming with curiosity.

"I date when it's convenient. How about you?"

"I don't date at all."

"I find that very difficult to believe. You're a beautiful, intelligent woman. I'm sure men are falling all over themselves trying to take you out."

"You think I'm beautiful?"

Nicholas laughed, the chortle gut-deep. "I thought you said you weren't vain?"

"How's that vain? I didn't say I was beautiful. You did."

"But you liked me telling you that you're beautiful."

"I didn't say that. I didn't say that at all."

"You didn't have to. I read your mind."

"So you're a mind reader now?"

"I am," Nicholas said matter-of-factly.

"That means you can tell what I'm thinking right now."

"Yep!"

"Well, don't keep me waiting."

"You're wishing that I was there…right now… and that I would kiss you."

"I'm thinking about you kissing me?"

"You are. You really want me to kiss you. One of my toe-curling, back-arching, tongue-twisting kisses that will make you weak in the knees."

Tarah's eyes widened as she stared at him, his expression smug and confident. She shook her head. "That's not what I was thinking about."

"Are you saying I'm wrong?"

Tarah giggled. "That's exactly what I'm saying."

"What were you thinking, then?" Nicholas asked.

"That it was time for me to say good-night. Sleep well!" she concluded, and then she disconnected their call, barely giving him a second to say it back.

Tarah sat upright, pulling her knees to her chest as she wrapped her arms tightly around her legs. She shook her head as she reflected on what Nicholas had said, hating to admit that the man had actually been right.

Those last days leading up to the final play-offs left Nicholas little time to think about anything but the game, yet thoughts of Tarah invaded every hour of his day. Between practice and the required pre-game events he was contractually obligated to participate in, the little downtime he had revolved around thoughts of her.

At the honors award banquet, he found himself wishing he'd flown her in to be his date on the red carpet. As he stood alone, paparazzi snapping picture after picture, he couldn't help but imagine her in black satin beneath a perfect formfitting red gown. Despite her best efforts to hide her assets, Tarah had a phenomenal figure, her dips and curves befitting any Parisian catwalk. He knew beyond any doubt that she would have been stunning on his arm and the talk of every news outlet across the nation.

Despite their best efforts, he had been able to grab only a quick few minutes with her on her cell phone, and he was itching to fire up his computer to see her in real time. Skype had become his new favorite pastime, and he was missing those moments they shared. Warm breath rushed past his lips as he slammed his locker door closed and headed out to the football field.

It was Media Day, and close to three thousand media members, armed with the requisite credentials, had descended upon both teams. It was a frenzy of photo opportunities and interviews. Each player was required to be available for at least an hour. They'd been calling his name for more than ten minutes, and he knew that it was only a matter of time before one or all of the coaches and a host of other officiates came looking for him. But as he stepped through the doors, the cameras beginning to flash over and over again, his head just wasn't in the moment.

Surgery had taken longer than anticipated, and everyone was waiting with bated breath. The next forty-eight hours would be crucial to the final outcome of the Barton twins. The team of surgeons that had been responsible for their care were all hopeful, and the prognosis for their recovery was better than good.

Tarah stared down at the two angels. They were both resting comfortably in separate cribs for the first time in their young lives. Their mother, Jessica Barton, sat between them, her eyes skipping back and forth, afraid that she might miss one or the other take a breath.

"Their stats are good," Tarah said softly, her voice

just above a whisper. "Both boys are doing really well, Mrs. Barton."

"Please, call me Jessica," the young woman said as she brushed a tear from her cheek. "What all of you did for my boys... I can't begin to thank you."

Tarah gave the woman a warm smile. "Is your husband still here, Jessica?"

She shook her head. "He ran home to get a quick shower. He should be back any minute."

"That's good. You should give yourself a break once he gets back. You need some rest, too."

She shook her head vehemently. "I'm not leaving them. I can't. I'd never be able to live with myself if something happened to either one of my babies and I wasn't here."

Tarah nodded. "I understand," she said. And she did, remembering how her mother had been when she or any of her siblings had fallen ill. But the minor mishaps and sicknesses they might have had didn't begin to compare to what little Oscar and Henry had endured. She imagined that when the day came that she had children of her own, she would be just as unyielding. "If you need anything, let the nurses know," she concluded. She brushed a gentle hand across the woman's shoulder and gave it a slight squeeze.

The two women exchanged a look before Tarah turned and exited the room. She returned the patient charts to the nurses' station after jotting down her notes and updating their stats for whoever might come behind her. The nurse on duty promised to find her if there was any change with either baby.

Tarah moved slowly down the length of corridor toward the physicians' on-call room. She was physically exhausted, her body beginning to cry for just a few minutes of sleep. The past two days had been everything she could ever have wished for, and she had learned quickly about the stuff she was made of. She imagined that she would have made Ma and Pa Boudreaux extremely proud. But before she could think about laying her head down to rest, she wanted to call Nicholas to wish him good luck before his big day. He was hours away from his first championship game, and she wanted him to know she was praying for his success and the elusive ring he coveted.

As she rounded the corner toward the hospital elevators, she almost ran headfirst into Dr. Harper. He was freshly shaven and had changed into a clean pair of scrubs. A few hours of sleep had done him good, and he looked well-rested. His eyes widened as he grabbed her shoulders, preventing what could have been a painful encounter for them both.

"Excuse me!" Tarah exclaimed, her own gaze filling with contrition. "I wasn't paying attention. I am so sorry!"

Dr. Harper gave her a slight smile, still holding tightly to her. "No harm done, Dr. Boudreaux. Are you okay?"

She nodded as she took a step back, extricating herself from his grasp. "I am. Tired. I was just going down to the doctors' lounge to close my eyes for a minute."

He nodded. "I was headed to the NICU to check in on the twins. How are they doing?"

"They seem to be doing really well. Both are resting comfortably, and they look great. Good color, normal temperatures and all their stats are at normal or acceptable levels."

"That's good to hear."

An awkward silence billowed between them. Tarah tossed a look over her shoulder and then took a deep breath. Dr. Harper was eyeing her intently.

"You should be very proud of yourself, Tarah. You're an outstanding surgeon. We were all impressed with your work today."

Tarah gave him a slight smile. "Thank you. I appreciate that, sir."

"We should make plans to celebrate. Maybe do dinner again later this week?"

"Will all the doctors be participating?"

He paused, his gaze narrowing ever so slightly. "Would spending time alone with me be such a horrible thing?"

Tarah shook her head slowly. "That's not at all what I meant, sir. I just…"

He interrupted her. "If you aren't interested in my attention, you should just say so, Tarah."

Tarah exhaled, releasing the breath she'd been holding, trying to resist the urge to run, or worse, throw a punch in the man's direction. She felt cornered, and she didn't like it. Taking another deep breath, she chose her words carefully. "Dr. Harper, I truly appreciate everything you've done for me.

You've been an outstanding mentor. And although I'm flattered by your attention, I am in a relationship. If I gave you the wrong impression, I apologize. That was never my intention. But I value your friendship, and I really hope that we can keep things from becoming awkward between us."

The man suddenly looked like he'd lost his very best friend. "I didn't know you were involved with anyone."

She nodded. "It's long-distance at the moment, but we're making it work. Work keeps him traveling, but he'll be here in a few weeks. I look forward to introducing you to each other."

Dr. Harper nodded. "I should be going. I need to check on my patients. If I'm around when you wake up, maybe we can grab a cup of coffee. In the cafeteria," he concluded.

Tarah gave him a slight smile. "Good night, sir," she said, and then he turned, stomping off toward the intensive care nursery.

When he was out of sight, she sucked in two quick breaths of air and blew them out gradually. She understood enough about men to know that her problem with Dr. Harper was far from over, but she was too tired to figure out what she needed to do to make things right again. She needed sleep and she needed to talk to Nicholas. Anything else would have to wait.

Minutes later, as she stepped off the elevator, she was dialing his number, her fingers crossed that she wouldn't wake him from a sound sleep. Nicholas answered on the second ring.

"Hey there!"

"Hey, yourself. How was your day?"

He nodded into the receiver. "Press, practice, more press. I need to get some sleep, but I'm too amped. How about you? How did the surgery go?"

"The twins are doing really well. I'd venture to say surgery was a complete success. The next few days will give us a better idea of what their quality of life will be like, but I'm very hopeful. They have great parents and a wonderful family pulling for them."

"That's my girl! I knew it would go well."

"I'm glad you did. I was scared to death, Nicholas. Their lives were in our hands, and if I or any of the other surgeons had made one mistake…well…"

"But you did it. And you'll keep doing it. Surgery is what you love, Tarah, so you don't have any option but to be the very best at it."

"I do love it!"

"You are something special, Tarah Boudreaux. All of your patients are blessed to have you."

Tarah felt her face pull into a wide smile. "Thank you, Nicholas. I appreciate that." A yawn suddenly escaped past her lips. "We both really need to get some sleep. I'm done, but you still have work to do tomorrow, and I expect a win," she said. "I just really wanted to hear your voice."

"I'm glad you called," Nicholas said, his voice dropping an octave.

"Me, too," she whispered back. "Can I call you

in the morning? What time are you headed to the stadium?"

"It won't be that early. Call or I'll try to call you before I leave."

"That'll work," Tarah said. "Sweet dreams, my friend."

Nicholas could feel a wave of warmth flood his body. "You, too, Tarah!" he responded, holding back the thought that his dreams would be very sweet because he'd be dreaming about her.

She called his name.

"Yes?"

"Tonight I told Dr. Harper I was in a long-distance relationship and that I had a boyfriend who I was exclusive with."

Nicholas grinned. "Okay."

She laughed, the sweet sound seeping through the phone line. "In case it ever comes up, I thought you should know."

"Will it come up?"

"When you come to Phoenix, should the two of you meet, he might think I was talking about you."

Nicholas laughed heartily. "So, you weren't talking about me?"

She laughed again. "In case it comes up," she said before she hung up the telephone.

Nicholas tossed his cell phone onto the nightstand beside the king-size bed. He lifted his long legs atop the plush mattress, settling into the pillows propped behind his back. He breathed in and out slowly, allowing his body to relax into the memory of the exchange he and Tarah had just shared. She made him laugh, and laughing lifted his spirits in ways he hadn't ever imagined. He liked her. He liked her a lot, and there had been no woman before her that he had ever felt that way about. He liked what he was feeling about Tarah, and what they shared out of the watchful eye of their family and friends had taken on a life of its own.

He was excited at the prospect of spending time with her and getting to know even more about her, and himself. His growing relationship with Tarah, the mutual moments of sharing himself, of letting his guard down and not being afraid of the vulnerability, had him learning much about the man he was. And even more about the man he hoped to become.

## *Chapter 6*

Nicholas and Tarah were able to Skype for over an hour before Nicholas had to pack up his gym bag and head to the stadium. It was four hours before the kickoff, and his nerves had already begun to curdle his stomach with anxiety. Tarah had teased him, and then she'd bowed her head and whispered a prayer of gratitude and thanksgiving. Before saying goodbye, she'd wished him the best of luck and had blown him a virtual kiss.

As he passed through the doors of the arena and headed into the locker room, he was feeling almost giddy with excitement and joy. A calm had enveloped him ever since the moment he'd heard her voice and seen her sweet smile.

Inside the locker room, the first thing he did was

find his assigned locker. His uniform and game day jersey hung inside. His name printed on the back of that customized jersey was telling. This was real. He was playing in the football league's biggest championship game. There was a moment when he couldn't begin to articulate what it all meant to him. As he tossed a glance around the room at his teammates, he realized they were all feeling some kind of way about their big day in football history. The energy in the room was subdued and focused.

Each of the players was indulging in his own personal game day ritual. There wasn't much else Nicholas felt a need to do, anxious only to get out on the field and play. But he moved to the training room area, the hub of activity. The list of last-minute pregame treatments being administered was lengthy, from massages to acupuncture. Some players were sitting for their customized tape jobs, white athletic tape being wrapped around ankles, knees and wrists. Stretching and loosening up was an ongoing process, and players were engaged in a host of activities around the room to make that happen.

Nicholas headed into the showers, standing under the spray of hot water until he felt cleansed and refreshed. When he was done and his favorite trainer had taped both his ankles tightly, he donned his game pants and shoes, then headed out to the field to survey the terrain.

Bare-chested, he took a slow lap around the track, making cuts into the turf to test the traction and ensure the spikes on his cleats were right for the surface. When he was satisfied, he moved back inside. He found his twin waiting for him, his brother more nervous than he was.

"Hey!" Nathaniel chimed. "How are you feeling?"

Nicholas nodded as the two clasped hands and bumped shoulders in a one-armed embrace. "I'm good."

"I'm not. My stomach is doing flips."

He laughed. "What are you anxious about? I'm the one who has to play!"

"That's why I'm nervous. I want this for you so badly!"

Nicholas smiled. "Did everyone make it?" he asked.

"The Stallions and the Boudreaux are all here. It's like a family reunion. I wish you'd been able to come meet us at the hotel last night. We all had a great time."

Nicholas nodded. "Me, too, but you know how I do. I just needed some alone time to get my head together. Plus, I did have that curfew!"

"It's all good. Everyone will be right here when the game is over, and we all have tickets to the celebration party tonight." Pride gleamed from Nathaniel's gaze.

"You ready to help me stretch?" Nicholas asked. He twisted his body at the waist, left and then right, before leaning his torso back and then forward.

Nathaniel nodded. "Whenever you are."

A perk of being the starting quarterback was the ability to handpick the support staff that helped him prep for the big games. His twin was an orthopedic specialist, and Nathaniel was all the help he had ever required or requested. Having his brother by his side always calmed him.

Moving into a quiet corner, Nicholas relaxed into his brother's touch as Nathaniel pushed and prodded each of his limbs, manually flexing and relaxing the tightness out of his muscles. As each sinewy tissue warmed from the manipulation, Nicholas found himself lost in thought.

This was his big moment. He tried to visualize himself making a big play, claiming the victory in his head. For a moment he imagined Tarah trying on his game ring dressed in nothing but his team jersey, her bare legs peeking from beneath the hem. The imagery made him smile as he thought about the moment he could make his fantasy come true.

By the time they were all ready to head out onto the field, dropping first onto one knee and bowing their heads for the team prayer, Nicholas could barely contain himself. Everything inside him promised a game that would go down in history, and he was ready for it. He had sacrificed a lifetime for this one moment. And he hoped that Tarah would at least be able to see the highlights on the television wherever she happened to be.

At halftime Los Angeles was behind, the score sixteen to thirteen. The New England fans were going wild. With less than three minutes left before halftime, Nicholas threw a long pass that connected beautifully in the end zone.

Tarah immediately called Katrina, shouting excitedly into the receiver. "Go, Mauraders!"

"Where are you?" Katrina questioned after requesting silence from their family sharing the VIP box so she could hear her sister.

"Headed to the hospital," Tarah said. "And I'm late, but I couldn't leave the house until halftime! Did you all see that throw?"

Katrina laughed. "We all saw it. Nicholas is playing really well."

"Nicholas is having a *great* game!"

Katrina paused for a split second before responding. "I thought you didn't like football?"

"I don't, but I like Nicholas, and he loves the game."

"Something you want to tell us?"

"Who's us?"

"Your family. His family."

Tarah laughed. "No. Why do think there would be something I need to tell?"

Katrina paused. "I hear it in your voice, baby sister," she then said matter-of-factly.

"Sounds like you're hearing things. Must be all that background noise."

"Uh-huh!"

Tarah giggled again. "I'll call back after the game. Tell everyone I miss them and give them a hug for me, please."

Katrina laughed with her sister. "Do you want

me to hug Nicholas for you? Maybe give him a kiss, too?"

"Goodbye, Katrina!" Tarah screamed into the receiver before disconnecting the call.

As she moved out of the faculty lounge and checked in on the Barton babies, Tarah knew she would miss the halftime show, but it couldn't be helped. The twins were sleeping peacefully, and as she reviewed their charts, she was pleased to see the few problems that had reared up since she last saw them were all minor. Oscar had run a low fever, and Henry's heart rate had been slightly irregular for a moment. But right now, everything was normal. Their mom and dad were smiling, both finally relaxing into all the good news and each accomplishment their infants were achieving.

After reiterating their care instructions to the nurse on duty, Tarah headed back down to the faculty lounge and the makeshift football party the nurses had coordinated for all the staff. Inside, there was a small crowd gathered around the television set. They were already at the end of the third quarter and the score was tied. Fans from both sides were hanging on the edges of their seats. Tarah could only begin to imagine what was going on in the minds of the other families who were actually there. She couldn't at all fathom what Nicholas had to be thinking out on the field.

She grabbed a paper plate and filled it with chips and spinach dip, then took a seat up front. As she sat down she noticed Dr. Harper for the first time, the surgeon seated on the other end of the front row. She gave him a slight wave of her hand and a bright smile. He gave her a quick nod, then turned his attention back to the conversation he was having with one of the orthopedic specialists about football and traumatic brain injury. They were the only two interested in the topic as everyone else was absorbed in the live game on the TV.

The cameras were focused on the players, and when a shot of Nicholas flashed across the screen, Tarah's smile spread full and wide. She couldn't have been prouder of Nicholas's big moment, and knowing just how much the game meant to him brought her immense joy.

The back-and-forth between the two teams was relentless. From all the comments in the room, it didn't take a brain surgeon to pick up on the fact that most were rooting for New England. None of them expected to see Los Angeles win. Tarah came to her feet in the fourth quarter. It was third down with five yards to go. The New England line had closed in on Nicholas, and he stumbled into the fray. When he suddenly rolled up and away, reaching back to fire a Hail Mary into his opponents' territory, she held her breath, not releasing it until the team's wide receiver jumped and landed, managing to grab the ball before stepping out of bounds. Everyone in the stadium roared and she jumped excitedly, cheering as if she were there. Los Angeles was within a few short feet of the end zone and their championship win.

The excitement was palpable. The play came with less than three minutes remaining in the game. Everyone was expecting Nicholas to throw another pass, but instead he sprinted left, then shifted with a hard right. Just as he dove toward the end zone he was hit hard from both sides, the impact slamming him over the line and down to the ground. The ball never left his hands. In the cheers and jubilation over the touchdown, seconds passed before anyone realized their star quarterback wasn't moving.

"What are they saying?" Tarah asked, still staring at the television screen. On the other end they had her on speakerphone.

"We don't know anything yet," Maitlyn answered. "Nathaniel, John and Noah ran down to find out what was going on."

Tarah nodded into the telephone. "Is Mason there?" she asked.

"I'm right here. Are you okay?" he questioned.

"I'm fine," Tarah said. "Tell Nathaniel the replay looks like Nicholas took the brunt of the hit in his lower spine and right hip. If he needs surgery, Dr. Harper is the best neurosurgeon in the nation. He said he can come there if necessary, but we have the best surgical team and facility here. Please, get Nicholas here to Phoenix Hope. Please! No matter what it takes! *Please!*"

For the first time ever, the family heard real panic in Tarah's plea. It was clear that she was holding back tears, the tremor in her tone edged with worry.

"I'll take care of it," Mason said softly. "I'll contact you as soon as we know something."

Katherine called her daughter's name from across the room. "Tarah, baby?"

"Yes, ma'am?"

"Do you have someone there with you? Senior and I don't want you to be by yourself right now."

"I'm at the hospital. I'm working. I'll be fine. I'll be better once I know Nicholas is going to be okay." Tarah stole another glance at the television screen, watching as paramedics wrapped a brace around Nicholas's neck. She paused for a moment as they eased a backboard beneath his body, then she resumed the conversation. "I'll call if I have any problems, Mom. Please, don't worry about me."

"We need to pray, Tarah. We need to pray for Nicholas, and we need to pray for all of our family."

Tarah nodded in agreement. She bowed her head, and as her mother lifted them all in prayer, a tear spilled from her eye.

Dr. Harper and Dana Harding were standing by Tarah's side when she disconnected the call. The doctor gave her a warm smile, and Dana reached out to squeeze her hand.

"I'm sure your friend will be fine," Dana said. "It just looks worse than it really is."

Tarah gave her a slight smile but she knew better. "I appreciate that. And I appreciate you offering to fly there to treat him," she said, shifting her gaze toward Dr. Harper.

He gestured with a slight tilt of his head. "I'm

sure they're going to take him to Mercy Hospital. I know one of the surgeons on their team. I'll call and see if I can find out anything," he said as he readied himself to leave.

"Thank you," Tarah said, her voice a loud whisper.

He brushed a large palm across her back. The touch was more intimate than friendly, and Tarah felt herself stiffen.

His hand moved from her back, snaking around her waist, and then he pressed his fingers along the side of her face, staring intently into her eyes. Tarah's gaze narrowed substantially, her jaw locked tight, her lips pulled into a deep frown. She drew her arms up and around her torso, hugging herself protectively.

"I'm here for you, Tarah. We all are," Dr. Harper concluded as he shot the nurse a look.

Dana smiled, her gaze skating back and forth between the two. She nodded her head in affirmation as her eyes locked with Tarah's. Her wide-eyed stare spoke volumes, the two women carrying on a silent conversation the doctor wasn't privy to.

Nicholas lay supine, his body strapped to a backboard and medical stretcher. His family was talking, but above everyone's voice he heard his brother's saying something he couldn't quite comprehend. His head throbbed and it felt better to keep his eyes closed, the bright lights shining on him not at all easy to take.

His entire body hurt, but he couldn't begin to pinpoint where the pain started or where it stopped.

Just that pain was there, in full regalia, like a high school band playing that one song with no intention of ever ending.

His decision to run that last offensive play instead of throwing it had seemed brilliant at the time. It hadn't been expected and it had won them the game. At least, that's how he remembered it. And then he remembered the pain that felt like it was coming with the proficiency of a drum line. Cymbals being slapped and horns blowing.

He tried to focus on the championship ring that would come engraved with his name and the new Cadillac that he'd earned as the game's MVP. Then he remembered that he'd lost out on his commercial opportunity, the cameras missing him telling the crowd that he was going to Disney. The advertising slogan, which was always broadcasted following championship games while a star player celebrated the team's victory, had become tradition.

For a moment his mind went blank, with nothing there but empty space. Then thoughts of Tarah Boudreaux billowed through the fog. Nicholas had imagined he'd heard her name from one of the many people around him. There was so much commotion, and he couldn't understand why no one would answer his questions. Then he couldn't remember if he had even asked any.

He wished he could contribute to the conversation, but words were lost to him. He wanted someone to call her. To tell her he was fine and would be all right. He imagined that she would be worried about him, and he didn't want her distracted with concern. He wished he could tell her himself that everything was going to be okay.

White dots danced behind his closed lids, and it felt like he was enjoying his own private light show. Then the room, or his body, or both, began to spin in a tight circle, the vertigo like a really bad amusement ride. It was suddenly hot and he felt as if he couldn't inhale any air.

Someone he thought to be Nathaniel told him to breathe, and when he did he realized there was a mask over his face and cool oxygen blowing up his nostrils. He tried to lift his hand, to wave his appreciation, but the straps were too tight around his arms.

He closed his eyes, then wondered when he'd opened them or if they'd actually been open the entire time. He struggled to gather his thoughts, to make sense of his situation. But when he couldn't, he let his mind go again, thinking only of Tarah, and football. He imagined her there, whispering in his ear, her soft cheek pressed against his, her warm breath like the sweetest song as he waited for her to laugh.

She was as beautiful as ever, and then she kissed him, her lips brushing lightly over his as she admonished him to rest.

Tarah was standing at the door to the hospital's helipad when the life flight aircraft landed. She'd been waiting since her brother had called to give her the update on Nicholas's condition.

After being transported from the football field to the hospital, he'd been assessed, stabilized, lightly sedated, put on a plane and flown from Minneapolis into Phoenix. According to Nicholas's brother, the preliminary diagnosis was a cervical spine injury with potential neurological deficits. But Tarah knew there was a host of things that needed to be sorted out before any definitive prognosis could be made. Nicholas needed a full neurological exam to assess his motor, movement and sensory functions. Only then would any doctor be able to give them a full diagnosis and predict his chance of recovery.

Her recommendation to transfer him to Phoenix Hope had been met with some reluctance. Dr. Nathaniel Stallion had not been wholeheartedly in agreement, concerned that moving his brother might do more harm than good. An extensive conversation with Dr. Harper and the neurological team at Mercy Hospital had helped change his mind. His understanding that the decision could very well mean the difference between Nicholas walking again or not had solidified the next steps.

Tarah watched as they lowered Nicholas from the plane, cautious about the monitors and tubes to which he was connected. As the medical team that had escorted him rolled his stretcher toward her, she suddenly felt her heart race, and her breath caught in her chest as she took a deep inhalation of air and held it. The staff meeting the flight pushed past her to help him inside. As they took a quick minute to assess his vital signs, Tarah moved to his side.

His eyes were closed and his breathing was slightly labored. She pressed her hand to his chest, feeling the beat of his heart against her palm. For just a quick moment she would have sworn that when she touched him, her own heart synced with his, the two tempos beating together evenly.

Leaning over him, she wrapped her arm above his head and dropped her face close to his. She pressed her cheek to his cheek, the sensation of his warm flesh against hers drawing tears from her eyes. She exhaled, and her warm breath gently brushed against his skin.

The sweetest breeze blew by Nicholas's nose, and the scent of vanilla and jasmine washed over him. He opened his eyes, his lashes fluttering, then closed them, then opened them again. He struggled to focus. Everything was distorted. *I must still be dreaming*, he mused. Then suddenly there was no doubt in his mind that Tarah was actually there and not a figment of his imagination. She was close enough to touch and smell, her signature fragrance wafting in the space around him. He felt himself smile as he whispered her name, the cadence of it falling like a feather past his lips.

Tarah drew the back of her fingers down the side of his face. "I've got you, Nicholas. I'm right here and I've got you," she whispered back.

Nathaniel and the rest of the family weren't too far behind, arriving some thirty minutes after life flight had departed for another trip. Everyone had flown in on one of the private planes owned by Noah's wife, Cat Moore. A sea of Stallions and Boudreaux practically ambushed the reception area, everyone anxious for information. Tarah met them at the door, hugs and kisses sweeping around the room.

"How is he?" Naomi asked, wringing her hands nervously. "No one's told us anything."

Her sister, Natalie, and Natalie's husband, Tinjin Braddy, pressed anxiously at her elbow.

"I need to see him," Nathaniel insisted. "I want to know what's going on. I need to be with him."

Tarah nodded. "The nurse will take you right on up, Nathaniel. Dr. Harper arranged for you to have full medical privileges while you're here but wanted to remind you that treating your brother would be a conflict of interest. Dr. Mingo is the orthopedic specialist on the medical team that will be working on Nicholas, and you are welcome to shadow him. He's waiting to talk to you when you're ready. Dr. Harper asked that if you disagree with any decisions about Nicholas's treatment plan, you speak with him directly."

Nathaniel nodded his appreciation. He lightly squeezed her elbow, then hurried behind the nurse, who gestured for him to follow. Tarah turned her attention to the Stallion siblings. "Nicholas is resting comfortably. He's sedated, and we'll be running a battery of tests on him for the next few hours. Once we get all the results back, I'll come talk to you."

"He's going to be okay, isn't he?" Natalie questioned. "Everyone's been talking in circles and using big medical words that none of us understands."

Tarah took a deep breath. The initial prognosis didn't look promising. Dr. Harper was still assessing Nicholas's injuries, but the consensus was that he might never walk again. But there wasn't enough information to tell his family that their brother was permanently paralyzed at that time. Despite all of her medical training, even she hadn't been willing to accept that idea.

She slowly blew out the breath she'd been holding. "Nicholas has a very long road ahead of him. He's suffered severe trauma to his spinal cord, and it's very serious. To explain it as simply as I can, the brain and spinal cord are made up of cells called neurons. Those neurons gather and transmit signals throughout the body. Signals that help us move, control our central nervous system, all kinds of things. Nicholas's neurons have been severely damaged." She paused and took a deep breath before she continued.

"Now, there are two types of injured neurons, ones that are dead and ones that are only stunned. Dead neurons can't recover. With the stunned neurons, if we can create the right environment for the spinal cord, they can return to normal and function again. Right now, we're trying to determine if his neurons can recover so we know exactly how to make that happen."

Noah moved to stand by his sisters. "Be honest

with us. Will he walk again? Nathaniel won't say, but we know he's concerned."

Tarah hesitated a second time. "We're going to do everything in our power to ensure a full recovery. And whatever we can't do, you all know God will."

"So we need to pray for a miracle," Naomi commented, her head waving from side to side. There was a hint of skepticism in her tone.

Tarah reached out and squeezed Naomi's hand. Tears misted the woman's eyes, and she swiped them away with her forearm.

Noah nodded his head in understanding. "Thank you, Tarah. We really appreciate everything you've done."

Tarah gave them a slight smile. "Someone will be down in a moment to take you all up to one of the family waiting rooms on the surgical floor. You'll be more comfortable there, and if you need anything, don't hesitate to ask."

As Tarah turned, she overheard chatter in the close distance.

"Wow!" Kamaya exclaimed. "Was that doctor our baby sister?"

"Our baby has really grown up," Maitlyn said. "And she's a doctor! I can't wait to tell Mom!"

## Chapter 7

Nicholas had gotten proficient at pretending to be asleep when the team of doctors came into the room. The drugs also helped. He let them talk among themselves as if he weren't even there. They debated treatment, argued tactics and were all genuinely concerned with his recovery. His family had come and gone a few times, always praying over him at least once each time. Sometimes Naomi cried and his sister rarely, if ever, let anyone see her do that. Natalie, on the other hand, bawled like a baby, reminding him of when they were younger and she was always crying about something. Noah was keeping them grounded, though, always taking his role as big brother seriously.

Since arriving at the hospital, they'd had to get

his blood pressure stable, and for a brief time, he had needed assistance breathing. He'd been given steroid medications to reduce the swelling of his spinal cord, and there had been a host of other tests done including X-rays, MRIs, CT scans and an ultrasound of his kidneys. They'd stuck him with pins to see how he responded to the pricks. He'd been made to try to move different parts of his body to test the strength of his muscles. After that, he'd closed his eyes and had pretended not to know they were in the room. He'd lost count of how many times every test, comment and gesture had been repeated.

Since that first day, he and Tarah had only one full conversation. He'd woken to find her by his bedside, eyeing him intently. Worry had creased her brow with the faintest line. As his eyes had adjusted, she'd smiled sweetly at him.

"You made quite an entrance," she'd said teasingly. "How are you feeling?"

He'd shrugged his shoulders. "It's all good, right? This is nothing but a fluke?" He gestured down to his legs.

Tarah had taken a deep breath, her expression shifting into business mode. Her tone had been controlled and even. "Let me give you my doctor spiel," she said.

His mouth had turned into a deep frown as he listened.

"You suffered an injury to your spinal cord. Your upper body is unaffected. You should have good trunk and abdominal muscle control. It helps that you were in great physical condition."

"I heard one of the doctors say it's paraplegia? That means I'm going to be in a wheelchair for the rest of my life, right?"

"Technically, what you have is a lumbar and sacral injury to your lower spinal nerves called cauda equina syndrome. That means you'll have decreased control of your hip flexors and legs. You may never walk or feel anything below your belly button again. That's correct."

"So is there a chance that I may feel something?"

"I can't say with any certainty. I'm just hoping you'll prove us all wrong. But that's going to require a lot of effort on your part. Most of your recovery will occur in the next six months. And as soon as we feel you're stable enough, we'll start rehabilitation."

"What good is that going to do?"

"The goal of rehab is to help prepare you for life after you leave the facility so that you can be as independent as possible."

He had pondered her comment for a moment, and then he'd turned his head away, sinking deep into a depression like he'd never known before. Angry at the world, Nicholas had taken his frustration out on Tarah. He'd been curt and distant, his sullen behavior bad at best. He'd found her bubbly personality off-putting because he couldn't see anything to be happy about. He brooded while she cheered. He was gloomy and she was the polar opposite. And although she hadn't been happy with him either, not once did she ever let it show.

Tarah had not concerned herself with his bad mood and even worse behavior. Pushing him to take control of his recovery became her mission as she interjected herself into his life on a daily basis, determined to support him. And then her antics had started.

Once they'd gotten him up and seated in a wheelchair, he had refused to cooperate, opting instead to stare out the window, wishing the hours away. Tarah had turned up every day right after lunch, cheerful and enthusiastic as she'd hijacked him and his wheelchair, taking him around the hospital campus and outside to get some fresh air. Her attentions had been steadfast and deliberate. Each and every time she'd drone on and on about her studies, her patients and what she loved about Arizona, starting with the heat. But despite everyone's efforts, Nicholas had been like ice, hard and cold.

Nathaniel had been there day in and day out, talking to him, motivating him, cheering him on and feeling immense guilt as if the accident had been his fault. Years earlier he'd prophesized something like this happening. It had been right around the time their brother Noah had reconnected with his high school honey. Catherine had fallen head over heels for the oldest Stallion's magic and was now his wife. Back then Nathaniel had advised him to retire and move on to something else before he wasn't able to move on to anything. Nicholas hadn't listened. At the time, too many unfulfilled dreams lingered in his head and heart.

Suddenly thinking about all his family made Nicholas smile, the first bend to his lips that had come since before his accident. The expression actually felt good, the muscles in his face feeling right again. Thinking back to his big brother, Nicholas had never fathomed any woman being able to get under his skin the way Catherine had gotten under Noah's.

He also hadn't believed that anything could have knocked him out of the game, changing the direction of his life. But he'd been wrong. Because he would probably never walk again. It had been a good run, and despite the hand now dealt to him, there wasn't much he could complain about.

He tried to sit upright. The effort required to drag his legs and pull his torso forward was exhausting. Tarah's warm voice suddenly sounded from the other side of the room.

"Why don't you use the buttons on the side of the bed to your left? You know you can incline your back and sit up that way, right?" she said as she moved to his side, leaning on the rail to stare down at him. "Would you like some help?"

Nicholas shook his head. "Hey there," he said, his voice low and slightly pained.

She smiled. "Hey, yourself. You really should take your time trying to talk. Your throat will be sore for a while from when we removed your ventilator."

He nodded, mindful of the emergency procedure

that had been necessary to help him breathe. "Are you going to give me a hand so I can sit up or what?"

"Finally tired of lying around pretending to be out of it?"

"Who said I was pretending?"

Tarah tossed him a look. "It's your lie. Tell it any way you want to tell it." She engaged the bed's remote and slowly lifted the back of it until his head was inclined upward. "And for the record, I'm really pissed off that you wouldn't talk to me before now. Playing sleep every time I came into the room was not cool. I'm just going to put that out here. I deserved better than that from you, Nicholas Stallion. You've been rude and nasty and haven't made any effort to excuse yourself for your behavior. But now I'm saying something. You really are not a nice guy!"

He took a deep breath as he reached out and grabbed the side rails with both hands. "Yeah, about that. I had a lot going on." He met the cool stare she was giving him, and his expression tinged with embarrassment. He couldn't admit that being in his head had gotten the best of him. It was a level of depression he had never experienced before, and he hadn't wanted Tarah to see him like that. He also hadn't trusted what might have slipped out of his mouth. So he hadn't really spoken to anyone, not even his twin, despite everyone's efforts to engage him. And now he was ready to move on, to be done with the pity party he'd gotten lost in. He knew his attitude would have a major impact on what his future held for him.

"You're really lucky I like you!" Tarah said while

rolling her eyes. "But I'm not giving you any more passes."

"And I don't expect you to. You've already done too much for me. I owe you!"

"Darn right you do! And I plan to collect. Trust that!" She winked at him.

Nicholas's eyes widened slightly. "I know this sounds stupid, but damn!" he exclaimed. "I really can't feel my legs!"

Tarah reached out and squeezed his hand. Her touch was warm and gentle, and Nicholas felt his breath catch deep in his chest. The look on her face was soothing. "It's going to take some time for you to adjust. You have a long road of rehabilitation ahead of you. But I'll be right here with you."

"You've got me, right? Isn't that what you said?"

"So you did hear me!"

He nodded. "I've heard everything everyone said. Everything *you* said, I trusted."

From the moment he was lifted off that plane, Tarah had been right there with him. Every free moment she had was spent by his side, watching him sleep, watching him struggle, even catching him cry a time or two. She hadn't pushed or intruded on any of those moments when he'd needed to be left alone. His brothers had pushed. His sisters had intruded. Tarah had just allowed him to be, her presence comforting and easy like an expensive cigar and an aged scotch.

He knew that she had her studies and her patients and her spare time was minimal, but she'd given him each and every second of that spare time, not once hesitating or doubting her decisions. Even when he'd been at his worst, spewing venom, everything about his presence ugly, Tarah had overlooked his bad behavior and evil temper. She had been a rock when he'd been at his weakest, and he trusted that whatever trials lay ahead for him, Tarah would have him. She would catch him if he happened to fall.

The two exchanged a look, and in that moment a spark of understanding seemed to flicker between them. It was significant, and both settled easily into the comfort of it. They were friends, and the bond of that alliance was like steel embedded in concrete.

"I'm sorry," Nicholas said. "I was horrible to you, and I couldn't blame you if you wanted nothing to do with me."

"I don't turn on people I care about," she said, finally shifting her gaze from his. "I understand you were going through some things. You just remember this moment, though, if the tables are ever turned and I start acting like a witch. You'll owe me a pass. Maybe even two."

Nathaniel stepped into the room, interrupting the moment. Dr. Harper followed on his heels, the two men in deep discussion. Both came to an abrupt stop at the sight of Nicholas actually sitting up slightly.

"What's going on?" Dr. Harper questioned, looking from one to the other. He moved swiftly to Nicholas's side, his stethoscope raised to check his patient's pulse and heart rate.

Nicholas chuckled, amusement dancing over his

face. "Dr. Boudreaux was giving me an update on my condition. It's the first time the drugs haven't had me woozy, and I had some questions."

Dr. Harper shot her a look. "You should have had me paged," he said matter-of-factly.

Tarah took a deep breath. "I've been here only for a moment, sir. And since I'm not officially on duty, I took that moment to have a private conversation with my boyfriend."

Dr. Harper bristled. His gaze swept from her to Nicholas and back. "Mr. Stallion is the boyfriend you spoke of. The one you said was coming to town?"

Tarah nodded as she gestured from one to the other. "Yes. Dr. Thaddeus Harper, Nicholas Stallion. Nicholas, this is Dr. Harper."

Nicholas laughed. "Neither of us anticipated me coming in with so much fanfare," he said. "I'm sure these weren't the circumstances any of us imagined meeting under."

Dr. Harper nodded, pretending to be occupied by his stethoscope. "Take a deep breath for me, please," he commanded.

Nathaniel's eyes shifted from his brother to Tarah. The hilarity of the moment had him fighting not to laugh out loud. He crossed his arms tightly over his broad chest. He and Tarah exchanged a look as Dr. Harper went into his own dissertation about Nicholas's condition, reiterating everything Tarah had said to him.

"Do you have any questions?" Dr. Harper asked.

Nicholas hesitated for a quick minute. "Yeah." he said finally. "How soon can I start rehab?"

"How long have you and Tarah been an item?" Nathaniel questioned, amusement dancing in his eyes. He dropped down onto the chair that Tarah had vacated just minutes earlier.

Nicholas shrugged. "We're not an item. We're just…well…" He shrugged again.

"She said you were her boyfriend."

"Dr. Harper's been sweatin' her for a while now. I'm a good cover. That's all it is."

"Cover, my ass! I see how you two look at each other!"

Nicholas shook his head. There was a moment of pause as he stared at Nathaniel. "It really doesn't matter anymore," he said, his voice low. "I would never want to put this on her."

"Put what on her?"

"All of this," he said as he gestured with his hand, his fingers fanning the length of his legs. "What kind of man can I be in a wheelchair? She deserves better. Tarah deserves a whole man, not one who comes with pieces that barely work if they even work at all."

Nathaniel narrowed his gaze. "What she deserves is a man who is going to love and respect her. Clearly, if she were concerned about your pieces working, she would let you know. I've gotten the impression that Tarah has never been shy about speaking her mind."

Nicholas cut an eye at his brother. "I don't

know…" His voice trailed off as his mind shifted into thought.

"What do you mean, you don't know?" Nathaniel questioned, eyeing him intently.

The brothers exchanged a look. Nicholas took a deep breath and held it for a moment before blowing it slowly past his lips. "Before my accident, I wouldn't have given it a second thought. I really like Tarah, and I wanted to see where we could take our relationship. But now…well… I feel like that window of opportunity has come and gone. It is what it is."

"What it is, is you feeling sorry for yourself. Tarah cares about you. She liked you before you hurt yourself, and she still likes you now. Don't count her out until she tells you she wants to be counted out. You need to talk to her."

Nicholas shook his head. "I appreciate the advice, but…"

"But nothing. *Take* the advice. *Please.* Do us both a favor and just have a conversation with her. Ask her how she feels and then decide."

For the next few minutes Nicholas and his brother eyed each other. Their conversation was telepathic, something to do with their twindom as they both argued their individual opinions with their eyes. Then Nicholas closed his, the gesture a sign of his acquiescing.

As Nathaniel stood up to leave, Nicholas called after his brother.

"Yeah?"

"I'm scared," Nicholas said, hot tears misting behind his eyelids. "I'm really scared, bro."

Nathaniel stood staring at him. "I know. I am, too."

Nicholas nodded his head, and then he closed his eyes and let himself drift off to sleep.

Dana Harding grabbed Tarah's hand and pulled her toward the women's restroom.

"What's the matter…?" Tarah started as she followed behind her new friend.

The two women had become close, bonding over their dislike of the hospital's head surgeon. Both were the youngest female children from large families. Both loved what they did in the medical profession. Neither liked shopping unless it was from behind a computer screen. Both had a reputation for being impulsive and spoiled, and the two were intent on proving their loved ones wrong. After taking all that into consideration, they were polar opposites. Dana loved hardcore rock and roll, and Tarah preferred country. Fast friends, they were having a great time bonding over their differences.

Dana shot a look over her shoulder. It was only after the door was closed and locked behind them and she was certain no one else occupied any of the other stalls that she spoke. "Dr. Harper! He's what's wrong!"

Tarah leaned her narrow hips against the sink. She groaned. "What now?"

"That man has it bad for you. He just figured out Nicholas Stallion is your boyfriend?"

"Technically, it's what I just told him. Why? Did he say something?"

"He hasn't stopped talking about it! He's said something to anyone who will take the time to listen to him. He's taking bets on how long you two stay together now that Mr. Stallion can't play football anymore."

"Please tell me he's just joking."

"Does it matter?"

"I swear that man is trying my patience. He really wants me to slug him!"

Dana laughed. "Don't hit him. We need great doctors like you around here. If you hit him, they'll make you leave, and he'll still be here making the rest of us miserable. Besides, I wouldn't want you to risk bruising your hand!"

Tarah took a deep breath and slowly shook her head. "He's just making it really hard. I don't know why he can't just accept he's been rejected and get over himself."

"Some men are like that. Dr. Harper has always gotten everything he's ever wanted. Except you. His fragile ego is seriously bruised."

"Well, I've got ninety-nine other problems to deal with right now, and his hurt feelings aren't among them."

Dana nodded. "How's Nicholas doing?"

Tarah shrugged. "He's hanging in there."

"For the record, I'm betting on the two of you making it."

Tarah smiled. "I appreciate the confidence, but

we're just good friends! There is nothing going on between us."

"Who are you trying to convince, me or you?"

"I'm serious. He's a great guy, but we don't know each other like that. Not really."

"Not yet. But you want to. I can see it on your face every time you talk about him."

Tarah snickered "You know better than anyone that I don't have the time to give to any man or relationship."

"Okay, if you say so!" A wide grin filled Dana's face.

Tarah shook her head. "I'm saying so."

"When are you on duty again?" Dana asked, changing the subject.

"I'm off for the next two days, but I'll be here early tomorrow to see the Barton twins head home. After that I'll be with Nicholas."

Dana laughed, and Tarah gave her a look. Dana held up her hands. "I didn't say anything!"

Tarah laughed with her. "But you were thinking it!"

Dana shrugged. "I'll find you for lunch tomorrow. We can run and get something from that little Mexican place if you have some time."

Tarah grimaced. "Let's do Chinese. And you can tell me about your date with the doctor from Cardiology."

Dana laughed. "Sounds like we'll be eating in the cafeteria again, because there's not much to tell!"

Exiting the restroom, the two women exchanged a quick hug and headed off in opposite directions. Tarah moved to the elevators, waiting patiently for the conveyor to stop on that floor. Her thoughts drifted to Dr. Harper's audacity to think it was okay to bet against her and Nicholas and what they shared when he didn't begin to have a clue. The man was blatantly disrespectful, and the next time they crossed paths, she would have no problem telling him so.

And then she thought about Nicholas. He wasn't her boyfriend, at least not officially. They had yet to have a serious conversation about what was going on between them. But there was no denying the bond they shared. There was something special between them, something neither understood nor could explain if they had to. But it was comfortable and easy, and they were both more than okay with it. Tarah reasoned that if it blossomed into something more, then perhaps it was meant to be, God having a hand in where destiny might take them.

Stepping out of the elevator, she pushed what some would call wishful thinking from her head. She walked toward the NICU, wanting to check on the twins. The duo was thriving, and she knew their stay was about to come to an end. When she arrived, a physical therapist was present, giving their parents instructions to help them continue to do well once they made it home.

Jessica waved at her excitedly, calling out her name.

"I didn't mean to interrupt," Tarah said. She moved to the young mother's side.

Jessica nuzzled one son against her chest, his bright eyes darting back at forth. "I'm glad you stopped by. We're leaving tomorrow!" she exclaimed excitedly. "Dr. Harper has cleared both boys to leave."

Tarah nodded. "I heard. I was actually planning on being here to say goodbye."

"I really want to thank you. My husband and I owe you so much for everything you did. You and all the other doctors."

"We really appreciate that. It means a lot to us!"

"So, we'll see you tomorrow?" Jessica asked.

Tarah's head bobbed eagerly as she reached for the second twin, pulling the infant into her arms. "I wouldn't miss it for anything in the world."

# Chapter 8

Nicholas smiled when Tarah entered his room. She was humming softly to herself as she stopped to check his charts for any new notes since the last time she'd been there.

It had been a good few months since his game-winning play, and Tarah had been there with him day in and day out as her time allowed. His friends, the coach, teammates and people he'd labeled casual acquaintances had visited as least once but not much more than that. The coach had delivered his winning ring and had assured him the team would be there to support him through his recovery. Nicholas had been grateful for the well wishes, but Tarah's dedication to his recovery was endearing, and he found her friendship invaluable.

Tarah was actually surprised to find him wide awake and alert, doing chin-ups on a utility bar that hung from the ceiling. "What's all this?" she asked.

"The physical therapy I asked for. Finally! A cutie named Maxine hooked me up."

Tarah smiled. "And Dr. Harper approved this?"

"Dr. Stallion and his new friends in the orthopedic department pulled some strings." Nicholas winked an eye. "I don't think the good Dr. Harper has been told yet!"

"So how's it coming along?" Tarah asked a wide grin across her face.

"I'm having a grand time learning how to do pull-ups!"

"Those pull-ups are going to help you move from this bed to a wheelchair. It's a step toward physical independence."

"About that. I was doing some research, and I ordered a few chairs I want to try. I'm having them delivered to your house, if that's okay?"

Tarah laughed. "Don't you think you might be moving a little fast?"

"Probably, but I have impulse control issues."

She shook her head. "You just like being a nuisance."

"That too!"

She moved to the side of the bed and sat down beside him. He dropped his torso back against the mountain of pillows that supported him and reached for his cell phone. Before Tarah could blink, Nicholas had wrapped an arm around her shoulder, pulled her close and taken a selfie.

"Hey! Really!" Tarah exclaimed. "What was that for?"

Nicholas laughed as he pushed buttons on his phone. "I'm posting a picture on my social media accounts. I need to get back in the game. Let my fans know I'm on the mend."

Tarah snatched his phone from his hand. She eyed the image of the two of them that he'd posted to his Instagram account. The caption read, The Girlfriend. It was not the most flattering image of her. She looked like a deer caught in the headlights, her curls askew, wearing her green surgical scrubs.

"This isn't cute," she said as she pushed the delete button.

"Hey, that was a good shot! I looked great!"

"If you're going to point me out, no one will care how you look." She pulled her thick hair into a high topknot, then pinched some color into her cheeks. Shifting her body closer against him, she held the phone at arm's length, centered them both in the screen and ordered him to smile. She snapped one picture and then a second. Choosing the better of the two, she posted it to his social media sites before passing the device back to him.

Nicholas laughed, reading her own caption. "Really? 'The best girlfriend in the whole wide world'?"

"You'd better believe it!" she said as she adjusted one of the pillows behind her head and back.

He grinned while shaking his head. "So, how is your day going so far?"

"It's been good. I had three surgeries this morning, and I performed a spinal fusion earlier this afternoon."

"So you're done for the day?"

"For the most part. I still have one patient in recovery, and as long as his vitals are stable for the next hour, I'll be able to release him to a room. Then I'll be done. I just needed to get off my feet for a minute."

"You need to go get some rest. Take a few days off, just crawl into bed and read a good book or something. You haven't taken a breather in months."

"I will. One day soon," she mumbled as she pulled her legs up, crossing them at the ankle.

Nicholas turned to stare at her. Her face was buried in a medical journal, focused on an article about electro studies on nerve regeneration. It was what he called serious reading, big words with too many letters and not enough pretty pictures. In the time it took her to blink she was completely lost in the text, everything around her fading into oblivion.

With a soft chuckle, he reached for the utility bar and went back to his efforts to pull himself up. Minutes later the sound of Tarah snoring vibrated through the room. Looking over his shoulder, Nicholas saw that she had drifted off to sleep, the medical journal having fallen into her lap. Her head hung down and to the side. Her mouth was parted just so, and he imagined that if she were left there uninterrupted long enough, drool would drip from her bottom lip. A loud snort slipped past her lips, and Nicholas couldn't help but laugh. Even in her sleep, she brought a smile to his face.

Allowing his torso to fall back again, he wrapped an arm around her shoulders, gently pushing and prodding until she lay straighter and looked more comfortable, careful not to disturb her rest. It was reflex that moved her to curl her body closer to his, leaning her head into his side. The nearness of her made his heart race, and he couldn't help but wish that things could be different for them. He brushed a stray curl from her face, his touch an easy caress. She was simply enchanting, and it amazed him that she didn't seem to have a clue just how remarkable she was. He sighed softly as he allowed himself to settle against her, slipping into the warmth of her body heat.

Tarah woke with a start, the alarm on the activity tracker on her wrist vibrating against her skin. She rubbed her hand against her eyes as she threw her legs off the side of the bed and sat upright.

Beside her Nicholas was sleeping soundly. He lay flat on his back, one arm thrown over his head. She had been lying against the other. His breathing was easy, his chest rising with each inhalation of air. Someone, probably his nurse, had cut off the bright lights in the room, leaving one fluorescent bulb on near the bathroom.

After adjusting the bedcovers around him, she leaned in and pressed the whisper of a kiss against his forehead. She smiled down at him as he muttered something about sandbags and ice cream. He sometimes talked in his sleep, and most times it didn't make an ounce of sense.

Tarah tiptoed out, needing to make one last round to check on her patients. No one had paged her, so she was fairly confident that all was well, no problems having risen while she slept. Being able to take that short power nap had done wonders for her. She headed out on her rounds with renewed vigor.

An hour later, Tarah had checked in on all of her patients, confirming that meds had been ordered and everyone was resting comfortably. She had just wished the last patient well when she stumbled upon Dr. Harper. He was standing in wait at the nurses' station, his eyes focused on a patient chart. When she spoke, greeting him politely, he shifted his attention in her direction.

"Dr. Boudreaux, you're still here?"

"I'm actually done for the day. I just checked on my last patient and handed over my charts to Dr. Weinstein."

Dr. Harper nodded. "I'm sure you were happy to hear that I'll be discharging your boyfriend."

Tarah's eyes widened in surprise. "Really?"

"Yes, I told him earlier today. I'm surprised he didn't say something to you."

Tarah smiled. "Actually, I was just headed up to see him now. You probably spoiled the surprise."

"My bad…" he said, a smirk pulling across his face. "I certainly didn't mean to do that."

"I'm sure you didn't," Tarah said, clearly not meaning a word that had come out of her mouth. Because she was certain that if Nicholas had been trying to surprise her, Thaddeus Harper would have done anything and everything to burst both their bubbles.

She turned abruptly, moving off in the other direction. Dr. Harper calling her name stopped her in her tracks.

"Yes?"

Dr. Harper smiled. He moved toward her until they were standing toe to toe. He gripped her shoulders with both hands. "Mr. Stallion is going to require a significant amount of attention once you get him home. If you find that handling him along with your responsibilities here at the hospital becomes problematic, please don't hesitate to let me know. I want you to know that I'm here for you. I'm here to help."

She eyed the doctor for a moment as she tried to ascertain if he was being genuine, and then she nodded her head. Turning away from his grasp, she moved quickly down the hallway, as far from the man as she could get.

Nicholas looked up to find Tarah standing in the doorway of his room. Her gaze was narrowed, an attitude seeping from her stare. He looked around as though he were searching for someplace to run and hide if it became necessary.

"What?" he questioned, trying to determine how

scared he should be, because clearly she was not a happy woman.

"When were you going to tell me?" Tarah asked, moving into the room and closing the door behind her.

His head tilted as he eyed her, understanding washing over him. "I was trying to find the right moment."

"You needed a right moment to tell me you were coming home?"

"About that… What had happened was…"

She moved swiftly to his side. "About what? Dr. Harper is releasing you and you didn't tell me. Do you know how I felt hearing it from him as he leered at me with that damn smug look on his face? Aargh!" she growled between clenched teeth. "One day smacking that *smug* look off his face is going to get me in some serious trouble!"

"Yeah, that wouldn't be good."

"Then I'm going to smack you!" she exclaimed.

Nicholas chuckled softly.

Tarah crossed her arms over her chest as she stared down at him. "You should have told me. There's a ton of work that needs to be done to get the house ready. It's a good thing I have the next few days off."

Nicholas sighed, warm breath floating past his lips. "I didn't want you worrying about that. In fact, I told Nathaniel to find me a small apartment some-where close to the hospital."

"Oh, no you did not!" Her hands fell to her hips, her head whipping from side to side.

"You look like that stereotypical angry woman right now."

"You did *not* just say that!" Tarah's eyes widened, her index finger waving in front of his face.

"Are we fighting? Because you look like you're ready to smack me, and I can't run. Remember? Non-functioning legs?"

"Aargh!" Tarah exclaimed, louder than the first time. "Are you really that kind of man? Really?"

"What kind of man is that?"

"The kind who makes decisions without talking it over with his partner! *That* kind of man."

He suddenly said haltingly, "Well... I... we... I didn't...*damn*."

"Don't cuss at me!" Tarah admonished.

"I wasn't... I..."

She cut him off. "There is no reason for you to get an apartment. There is plenty of room at my house for you, and I'll be there to help. You are not going to some apartment. I can't believe you'd think I'd let that happen or you could just make that decision without talking to me about it!"

"I'm sorry?"

"You should be!" Tarah dropped down onto the bed beside him. "Don't do it again."

The two sat in silence for a good few minutes. There was activity happening in the hallway outside his door that they both ignored as Nicholas reflected on their conversation and Tarah's reaction.

He reached for her hand and held it, entwining her fingers tightly between his own. "I really am sorry," he said as he felt her finally relax into the moment. "But I thought it would be best for both of us. With my own apartment, I'd be close, but I wouldn't be a burden to you. You've been such a great friend to me that I didn't want to put anything else on you."

"That's not your decision to make without talking to me first. We really need to work on our communication."

He chuckled softly. "Okay, then let's talk."

There was another moment of pause as they sat staring at each other. Tarah finally broke the silence.

"I care about you, Nicholas."

"I care about you, too. You've become my best friend."

She smiled. "But are we *more* than friends? I know we laugh and joke and tease each other, but how do you really feel about me? Am I a girl *friend*? Or am I *your girlfriend*?"

He took a deep breath. "I wanted you to be *my girlfriend*, but with the accident and everything… well… I didn't think…"

She narrowed her gaze. "We're not talking about your accident, or your legs, or any of that right now. What I need to hear is how you feel about me."

Nicholas shook his head. "But my legs and my medical problems are going to impact everything that will happen to us from this point forward. So you don't get to ignore it no matter what I feel for you or what you feel for me. That is not how this is going to work, Tarah. I'm sorry."

"Fine. But you still haven't answered my question. How do you feel about me?"

Nicholas sat taller. His eyes dropped down as he played with her fingers, gently caressing each one slowly. "You have become the most important person in my life. I want you to be happy more than I want anything else in this world. Even more than I want functioning legs. That's how much I care about you, Tarah." He lifted his gaze to meet hers, their eyes locking tightly as they stared at each other.

"Well, it took you long enough," Tarah answered, unbridled joy shimmering in her tone.

Nicholas continued. "And because I care about you so much, Tarah, I'm not going to let you just decide to become my caretaker and protector without knowing what you're getting yourself into. There is no way I'm just going to let you throw your life away when I know you deserve better than what I have to offer you right now."

"Make no mistake, Nicholas Stallion, I am fully aware of what I'm getting myself into. I know your medical needs better than you do. And I also know that if I didn't think you were worth whatever sacrifices we might have to make as a couple then I would have been upfront about that from the beginning. I never saw being with you as throwing my life away, so you need to check yourself with that."

"So you do care about me like that?" Nicholas's grin was miles wide.

"You have to ask?"

"No. I know you're falling in love with me."

Tarah narrowed her gaze in his direction. "I thought I told you not to cuss at me!"

"Who cussed?"

"You said the L-word."

"You really do have commitment issues, don't you?"

Tarah laughed. "Not at all, because I'm very committed to you."

Nicholas smiled. "Really?"

His eyes were dancing over her face, the look he was giving her like the sweetest caress. Tarah inched her body closer to his. She pressed a hand to his chest as she leaned in, her face just millimeters away. Something delightful gleamed from her stare, and he found himself falling headfirst into the wealth of it. Nicholas felt the air catch in his chest as he took a swift breath and held it. And then she kissed him, pressing her mouth sweetly against his.

Despite what many people thought they knew about her, Tarah had not had that many first kisses. In fact, she could count on one hand the number of first kisses she'd had in her lifetime and have fingers left over. Tarah had often come across fast and flighty, but the men she dated would probably attest to her being rather stingy with her treats.

But kissing Nicholas felt like Christmas had come again and she'd gotten the biggest gift under the tree. She felt him snake an arm around her waist as he pulled her closer to him, his lips gliding like silk against hers. He tasted of chocolate pudding and peaches, the desserts he insisted on having with his dinner each night. His mouth was sweet and warm, and everything about that moment was as near perfect as she could begin to imagine a first kiss being.

When they finally broke the connection, a tear had fallen from his eye, dampening his cheek. Tarah touched her lips to the moisture, wiping it away with the tip of her tongue. She pressed her cheek to his, her skin warming his skin, then wrapped her arms around his neck and hugged him tightly.

There was something about Nicholas that moved her spirit like no other man had before him. She didn't have the words to describe what she was feeling for him, only that she had never before experienced the emotion that consumed her when he was in her head and heart. She wasn't ready to put a real label on what they were sharing, and she definitely wasn't ready to think about ever letting it go.

Minutes later she kicked off her shoes and crawled into the bed beside him. They held each other, trading easy caresses. As they talked, the conversation wafting from serious to silly and back again, laughter bubbled over. Tarah found that plotting and planning were a mutual give-and-take and a moment of self-discovery for them both. Hours later, when the late night nurse came to check on her patient, Tarah stirred, but Nicholas slept soundly by her side, still holding her hand tightly.

## Chapter 9

Tarah and Nicholas had settled into a comfortable routine with each other. For her, the hospital, her studies and her patients consumed a sizeable amount of her time. For him there was occupational therapy, psychotherapy and his personal favorite, robotic walking therapy with an exoskeleton robot that moved his legs.

In the evenings, or sometimes in the morning, depending on Tarah's schedule, they would enjoy the luxury of each other's company. They were discovering the music each other liked, an eclectic mix of his favorites and hers played daily throughout the home. Scrambled eggs and chopped salad had become a staple in their diets, the only things Tarah could cook well. Often they were supplemented by the gourmet meals Nicholas had delivered from a local food service and the fast food Tarah insisted on.

They both had a growing collection of books that they read voraciously. Tarah's were usually medical journals and science studies. Nicholas had grown fond of mysteries and suspense thrillers. They had also encouraged each other to read at least two passages from the Bible daily before they fell asleep each night.

They played cards and board games, and when they had no need for distractions, they simply relaxed in the quiet, listening to each other breathe. Although figuring out how he could be the best man he could be without the use of his legs was daunting, Nicholas appreciated Tarah being there to encourage him.

She tossed him a look from her seat at the dining room table. "What are we eating?" she asked, pushing the food on her plate with her fork.

"It's a couscous and arugula salad."

"Why are we eating this again?"

"It's been proven that an organic diet aids in cellular regeneration. So we're eating it because it's good for the both of us."

Tarah stared at him blankly, batting her eyelids over and over again. "It tastes like dirt."

"It does not taste like dirt."

"Actually dirt would probably taste better than this." She pushed her plate aside. "I'm going to order some burgers," she said as she stood up. "And fries."

"I'll take a chocolate milk shake with mine," Nicholas said as he pushed his own plate away.

Tarah laughed. "I thought you wanted to eat the dirt."

"I wanted to eat healthy."

"Trust me," Tarah said, her tone facetious, "clean eating is really overrated."

Nicholas laughed with her. "I cannot believe you just lied to me!"

"That was not a lie. A little fib, maybe."

"Did I tell you I hired a trainer?" Nicholas asked after Tarah had called for delivery from a local burger joint.

She sat back down in her seat, pulling one leg up beneath her bottom. "What do you need a trainer for?"

"I plan to compete in next year's Paralympics. It's a paratriathlon that includes a seven-hundred-fifty-meter swim, a twenty-kilometer ride on a hand cycle and a five-kilometer race in a wheelchair. And I plan to win."

Tarah reflected on his statement for a minute. Nicholas had made incredible strides since being released from the hospital. He'd regained his upper body strength, enabling him to push and maneuver his own wheelchair. Everyday activities were no longer a challenge. He dressed and bathed himself, got in and out of the car with no help and was determined not to be dependent on anyone if he didn't need to be. His swim, run, race thing would be a piece of cake.

She tossed him a nod of her head. "I'll be at the finish line to cheer you on, but I really don't know why you like to do things that make you sweat!"

He laughed. "Sweating is good for you. It cleans out your pores."

Tarah's expression was smug as she turned her attention to the sound of the doorbell ringing. "Real food!" she exclaimed as she rushed to answer the door.

"Look who I found," she said minutes later as Nathaniel followed her into the room, carrying their bag of burgers and fries.

"What's up?" he said to his twin as he dropped the delivery onto the table.

Nicholas bumped fists with Nathaniel. "Tarah was just telling me how much she isn't enjoying our organic diet."

Nathaniel pulled a fork full of his brother's couscous to his lips. He grimaced. "Yuck! I'd say she's probably made her point."

Nicholas shrugged. "What's going on with you?"

"I'm heading back to California," Nathaniel said. He shifted his eyes toward Tarah, then back to his brother.

Tarah grabbed her burger and fries. "I've got some calls to make," she said. "I'll give you two some privacy."

"You don't have to go," Nicholas said.

Nathaniel nodded his agreement. "Don't go on my account, Tarah."

She shook her head. "It's all good. You two talk. I'll be back in a few minutes."

Nathaniel took a seat as Tarah made her exit. He and Nicholas were alone together.

"Why are you leaving?" Nicholas asked, turning his eyes on his brother.

"It's time. I need to get back to my practice. So I'll be here until the end of the week, and then I'll be flying back home this weekend. Besides, you're doing just fine without me, so there really isn't any reason for me to stay longer."

Nicholas nodded. "I am doing well. In fact, I was just telling Tarah I think I'm going to train for the Paralympics."

His brother's eyes widened. "That's an impressive undertaking."

"It'll give me something to do."

"How are things with you and Tarah?" Nathaniel asked, tossing a quick look over his shoulder toward the door.

His brother smiled. "We're good, but since you asked…" He rolled himself to his brother's side, leaning in to whisper, the gesture conspiratorial. "What can you tell me about sex?"

Nathaniel grinned. "Didn't Noah have that talk with you when we were ten?"

Nicholas gave his brother a look, not at all amused. "That's not what I mean." This time he glanced toward the door, dropping his own voice another octave. "I had an erection yesterday. It lasted only about ten seconds but…well…" He was suddenly embarrassed, color flooding his face. "I didn't think that it would ever work again."

Nathaniel nodded. "Obviously I can't say for certain if you can or can't, but I know that in your situation, an erection is a good sign."

Nicholas grinned. Despite things going well between Tarah and him, he'd been keeping her at arm's length, questioning whether or not he would ever be able to have a romantic relationship with any woman. But Tarah excited him. Everything in his head and his heart still worked just fine. She tended to be overly affectionate, and he'd been surprised by the rise of nature that pressed taut in his pants when she'd hugged him goodbye the day before. It had been the first time his body had reacted since his accident, and it had also been the last, with nothing else happening since.

Nathaniel leaned in to whisper with him. "You need to talk to your doctors. If you're feeling some sensation, that's a very good sign, and there are things they can do to encourage that. If you're getting an erection but you're not able to maintain it, there are sexual enhancement pills that might work for you."

"You mean Viagra?"

"That's one of them. "Have a conversation with your urologist and see what he says. He'll probably have to run some more tests, but I'm sure they'll be well worth it in the end."

Anxiety and frustration about whether or not he could still *do it* had been plaguing Nicholas for weeks. He'd actually worried that sexual pleasure was a thing of the past, that he might not ever father children or that Tarah would find him undesirable and less of a man. His brother's advice had him hopeful.

Tarah interrupted the moment as she reentered the room. She eyed the two of them, a wry smirk pulling at her mouth. Curiosity danced in her gaze. "What are you two whispering about?"

"We are not whispering," Nicholas quipped. His face flushed with color, embarrassment tinting his cheeks a deep shade of ruby red. "Why are you being so nosy? I can't believe you're out there in the hallway eavesdropping!"

Tarah stared at him, her hands clutching her hips. "Don't get it twisted, Nicholas Stallion! I don't eavesdrop! And I don't appreciate you getting snippy with me just because you sprouted a boner and didn't know what to do with it!" A bright smile filled her beautiful face.

Nicholas's mouth lifted in a slow grin, his eyes locking tight with hers. "I'll have you know, Tarah Boudreaux, that *knowing* what to do is *hardly* my problem, so get your facts straight."

Tarah smirked, returning the look he was giving her with a narrowed gaze. "Then it sounds to me like there's something you and I need to be talking about."

Nathaniel choked back laughter, amusement dancing a mean two-step between the three of them. He suddenly rose from his seat. "On that note, I think I'll say goodbye."

Nathaniel had been gone for over an hour, and Nicholas and Tarah hadn't spoken to each other. It felt as if a wall of tension had risen thick and full between them.

Tarah had walked out onto the patio as Nicholas had finished his burger and fries. After clearing away his own dishes, he joined her, wheeling himself out to the pool. Tarah tossed him a look and a smile.

"I really didn't mean to eavesdrop on the conversation you were having with your brother," she said, contrition painting her expression.

He shrugged. "Yes, you did! But it's no big deal."

Tarah laughed. "Well, maybe I did. I was headed back to the dining room and, well…you know the rest."

Nicholas laughed with her. "So are you ready to talk?" he finally asked, his expression turning somber.

There was a moment of hesitation. "What I really want to do is dance!" she exclaimed as she threw her arms out to her sides and spun around in a circle.

She was wearing a floral print sundress that billowed around her petite frame. Her feet were bare, and Nicholas realized that it was one of the few times he had seen her in something other than her hospital scrubs. She looked comfortable and happy, her face glowing with sheer joy.

Nicholas stared at her, and then he nodded. He gestured for her to follow as he rolled himself back into the house. Minutes later, an old R & B song echoed out of the speakers.

Tarah stood watching as Nicholas wheeled back to her side, holding out his hand. Confusion washed over her expression as she slid her palm against his.

And then he pulled her down onto his lap, moving her to laugh with abandonment as she settled against him. As she wrapped both arms around his shoulders, he nuzzled his face into her neck, one hand spinning the wheelchair in a slow circle as the other held her close against him.

They danced. Their sensual connection was magnetic as he glided her around the room, his fingers trailing a slow path across her bare arms and shoulders. Tarah's eyes were closed as he pressed a line of damp kisses against her neck, his warm breath blowing along the line of her profile to the indentation of her dimples and up to the curve of her earlobe. He plunged his tongue into her ear and she gasped loudly, heat sweeping deeply into the pit of her abdomen.

"You're a tease," she whispered, her voice coming in short gasps.

"Am I?" Nicholas whispered back.

Tarah nodded as she pressed her palm against his chest, her fingertips igniting a wave of heat between them.

"I really want to make love to you, Tarah," he said. "You don't know how much I wish I could make that happen."

"You will," she said softly. "It will happen when it's supposed to."

"What if it doesn't? What if I never regain any functionality?"

"Nicholas, the act itself is only one third of the pleasure. One third is the experimenting, trying new things, the excitement and anticipation over what something might feel like. And the final third is knowing that your partner loves you enough and cares enough about you to want to try those new things with you."

"So, do you think about it? Do you think about what you're missing? Or that you may never have children with me? Does it ever cross your mind?"

Tarah pressed her forehead to his. "I do think about making love to you. I fantasize about it all the time. Every time we touch. When you make me laugh. When we fall asleep at night, I imagine what it will be like to feel you inside me. Thinking about you like that excites me. It gives me hope about what we might one day share. But I don't worry about it never happening because I know that it will, in some form or fashion. You are worrying for no reason at all."

"You don't worry enough! We're talking about your future, Tarah."

"No, we're talking about *our* future. Neither one of us is in this alone, Nicholas. We're in this together. At some point you really need to trust that."

Nicholas wrapped both arms around her and hugged her tightly. His hands fanned the length of her spine. Hearing her words was one thing, but believing them was something else altogether. But he did trust her. And he desperately wanted to believe that she was right.

As if she could read his mind, Tarah stared into his eyes, seeming to fall hard into the look he was giving her. Tarah kissed him then, her mouth claiming his possessively. Her tongue teased the curve of his full lips, peeking past the line of his teeth to play a game of give-and-take with his tongue. Kissing Tarah had become his favorite thing to do, and each and every time felt like the very first time.

It was an old school love song that played sweetly in the background. The sound was sexy and teasing, an electric guitar and a deep bass complementing the melody. Nicholas resumed their dance, Tarah cradled tight against his lap as he inched his chair around the room. He became lost in the moment, a mile-long playlist teasing his senses as a full moon rose high in the late night sky.

It had been a long workday. When Tarah finally found her way back home, she expected to find Nicholas sound asleep. She was surprised when he called her name as she tiptoed through the door, kicking off her rubber-soled heels in the foyer.

"Hey, what are you doing up? It's so late, I just knew you were going to be asleep!"

He smiled as she moved to his side to kiss his cheek. "I was waiting for you. How was your day?" Nicholas asked.

She pulled a chair up to him and sat down, then kicked her legs out and twisted her ankles from side to side. "I had only three surgeries today, but I don't think I had a chance to sit down once."

"Did you eat? I saved you some dinner."

She nodded. "I grabbed an egg roll and a container of egg drop soup from the Asian market by the hospital. I'm good." She grinned, her snow-white teeth shining bright. "What did you eat?"

"I actually cooked. I grilled pork chops and made a salad."

"You cooked? I'm impressed! If I'd known that, I would have waited until I got home to eat."

"I packed the leftovers for your lunch tomorrow, so you'll get to taste just how good my meal was."

"I'm impressed again. You're becoming quite the homemaker."

Emotion seemed to drain from Nicholas's face as he pondered her comment. He lifted his eyes to hers, the connection seeming to transfer the feelings.

"I'm sorry," Tarah said softly. "I didn't mean that as an insult."

Nicholas chuckled softly. "I wasn't insulted. This just wasn't the plan I'd imagined for myself."

"I did. For me, I mean. I always knew I'd be a big-time surgeon, and every night I'd come home to the hubby and kids. Dinner would be on the table and the laundry would be done. After homework, bedtime stories and prayers, my favorite guy and I would sit back, relax and trade war stories."

He laughed. "War stories? Really?"

"Yeah, how he and the science teacher went toe-to-toe about Junior's classroom behavior and the tea party my Mini-Me made him sit through when he wanted to watch the game on television. And I'd tell him about a patient who thought I was a nurse and not the surgeon and the doctor who underestimated my surgical skills and had to be schooled. Every day we'd have stories to share so that neither one of us would feel like we were missing anything."

He grinned. "I'm impressed with that vivid imagination of yours. You have it all figured out."

"I did. And now that I know who my partner in crime is going to be, it adds a whole new dimension to what I've been imagining." She slid her fingers between his, interlocking their hands together. The skin on his palm had begun to thicken, calluses growing from the work he was putting in with this wheelchair.

Nicholas's face gleamed with amazement. "I have a funny feeling I'm going to enjoy trading war stories with you."

Tarah leaned forward and pressed a gentle kiss against his lips. "I don't have to go to work tomorrow," she said as she broke the connection. "And I'm not sleepy. Do you want to watch a movie?"

He shook his head. "Let's just talk. I like when we talk."

She nodded. "First, did you make any dessert?"

Nicholas laughed. "Brownies are on the counter. I'll take mine with vanilla ice cream, please!"

Hours later, Tarah found herself still knee-deep in conversation, having moved from the living space to the master bedroom. The windows were wide open, a warm breeze blowing the sheer curtains about. Nicholas was propped against a mountain of pillows as she sat in a corner chair, her legs pulled beneath her bottom. She sipped on a warm cup of herbal tea, the oversize mug clasped tightly between her palms.

"So," Tarah said, her tone teasing, "when you look at a woman, what is the first thing you notice?"

"I'm an ass man. Hips and whips, baby!"

"When we first met, you were looking at my ass?"

"Nope! Your smile. *You* had the most beautiful smile."

Tarah grinned.

"And you were wearing the hell out of that dress you had on!" he added.

She smirked, emotion shimmering in her eyes. "Do you think it's okay to keep noticing other women after you are in a committed relationship?"

"I'll be married, Tarah, not dead! My turn. Do you masturbate?"

Her eyes widened. "My vibrator was my best boyfriend for many years," she said as she explained about her celibacy and her decision to abstain from sex until marriage.

"You're telling me that if I hadn't had my accident, we still wouldn't be having sex?"

"Not until our wedding night." Tarah grinned.

"And you had the audacity to call me a tease?"

Her laughter resonated deep into the core of his soul. "It is still going to be the best night of your life!"

Nicholas laughed with her, his head shaking from side to side.

"Since we're asking, do you masturbate?" Tarah asked.

Nicholas gave her a smug grin. "I was drafted to play pro-ball right out of college, remember? I had endorsement deals with sneaker companies, wineries and multiple men's fashion lines. I hung out with the rich and famous, and most of them were extremely beautiful women from all around the world. Masturbation was never necessary. Now it does nothing to help."

"When's your next appointment with your urologist? We should go talk to him together."

He nodded his head in agreement, his eyes drifting off into thought before he spoke again. "What is the one thing that would be a relationship breaker for you?"

"Infidelity. I can't stay with a man who can't be faithful to me."

"That won't be a problem."

"Emotional infidelity is just as bad. It doesn't always have to be physical. If you become emotionally connected to another woman, sharing your feelings with her when you should be sharing them with me, there's going to be an issue."

"Point taken."

Tarah paused for a moment. "What were you thinking about right before we kissed for the first time?"

"That you smelled like antiseptic."

Tarah's laugh was gut-deep, rising from deep in her midsection. "Was it that bad?"

"No. You also smelled clean and fresh. You reminded me of sunshine and vanilla bodywash!"

"Good save!"

"That was good, huh?"

The mirth between them was abundant, every

bit of it feeling as right as rain after an abundance of drought. The look Tarah gave him was teasing, her eyes narrowed seductively as she stared at him. Nicholas suddenly realized his breathing was short, coming in heated gasps. She bit down on her bottom lip, and he felt the heat surge deep into his core. He missed the sensation of an erection, hating that the faint twitch of muscle between his legs wouldn't amount to much of anything. He shook his head.

"What?" Tarah asked, concern simmering in her gaze. "What's wrong?"

"Nothing." He shook the sadness away. "If I asked, would you let me touch you?"

"Are you asking?"

"Maybe."

Tarah shifted forward in her seat. "Exactly what is it you're looking to touch?" she asked, her voice dropping slightly.

A slight smile pulled at his full lips. "You have beautiful...curves. I would really like to just hold them in my hands. Maybe let my tongue dip into your belly button while my fingers...well...dipped a little lower." He winked at her. "I'd also like to pull my hands through your hair, maybe even tug on it a time or two."

"You like to play rough?" Tarah giggled.

His smile widened, his eyebrows lifting suggestively. "As rough as you want me to."

"Sounds like we have much to look forward to," she said softly.

"So you'd let me touch you?"

"The day I become Mrs. Nicholas Stallion, you can touch anything you want. This will all be yours!" she said, her hands fanning across her body.

Nicholas laughed. "Tease!"

Tarah chuckled with him, and then she yawned widely, hiding the gesture behind her open palm. "Excuse me!"

"Don't do that. You know it's contagious!" he joked as he mimicked her.

Tarah rose from her seat and rested her mug on the nightstand. Then she crawled into the bed beside him and he wrapped his arms tight around her torso. "Are you tired?"

She nodded as she rested her head against his chest, her hand pressing over his belly button. "I am," she whispered, her eyes fluttering open and then closed.

Nicholas reached to turn off the light by his side of the bed. "One more question," he said.

"Yes?"

"When are you going to say that you love me?"

She lifted herself up slightly to stare down at him. Moonlight reflected across his face, shadows flickering back and forth. His expression was intense, the light searing his dark eyes. "I say it every day. At least I try. I might not say it with those words, but I definitely work hard to say it with my actions."

"Why are the words so hard for you?"

Tarah paused, pondering his question. "That was *two* questions," she finally said, deflecting the conversation. She rested her head back against his chest.

A wide smile filled Nicholas's face. He brushed his hand across her shoulder and pressed a kiss to her forehead. "Good night, Tarah," he said.

"Good night." She cradled her body against his, settling down for the night. It was only a matter of minutes before her breathing eased, the inhalations deep and slow, slumber beginning to take hold of her.

He kissed her forehead one last time. "I love you, Tarah," he said softly as he closed his own eyes. "I love you more than anything else in this world."

She smiled, and then she whispered back, "I love you, too, Nicholas. Heart and soul. Now and always."

Nicholas grinned into the darkness, allowed the words to swell like a balloon inflating around them. And then he laughed, Tarah's last comment bringing him immense joy, that balloon now sailing sky-high.

"And now that we got that out of your system, I hope we don't need to revisit it again. If we do, then I think we'll need to address your insecurity issues. But we'll have to bring in some help then, because that's not my specialty. They have other doctors for that."

"I think I'm good," he said, still chuckling warmly.

"You should be. You are the only man who has ever heard those words come out of my mouth."

"So, are you ever going to say them again?"

"I'll have my moments."

Nicholas said, "I appreciate the warning!"

Tarah gave him a light squeeze, and he hugged her close, tightening the hold he had on her as they both drifted off into the sweetest dreams.

## Chapter 10

"Do you love him, Tarah?"

Tarah smiled. Her mother's question was unexpected. They had been talking about work, catching up on family news, and Tarah had asked for her mother's baked spaghetti recipe. The question had come on the heels of her telling her mother that Nicholas wasn't a fan of canned tomatoes.

"Because it sounds like you've fallen in love with this young man, baby girl!" her mother proclaimed.

Tarah took a deep breath. "Nicholas is very special, Mama, and he makes me feel special. I do love him. I love him so much."

"And how does Nicholas feel about you?"

"He tells me he loves me every day, and I believe him."

"I'll be honest, baby. Your father and I had some concerns when you insisted Nicholas move into that house with you. His medical problems are a lot for a person to take on, and we were worried that it might distract you from your goals. Senior even told Mason to tell you no, but you know your brother!"

Tarah smiled again, making a mental note to call her eldest sibling to say thank you. Since the day she'd been born, she'd been able to count on Mason for everything. He had claimed her as his baby, and there had been nothing she had ever wanted that he had denied her. She didn't show her big brother nearly as much appreciation as he deserved. "Mason *adores* me!" she exclaimed.

"Mason *spoils* you!" Katherine laughed.

Tarah laughed along with her mother.

Her mother continued. "Your daddy was fascinated with that young man the last time we were there. Nicholas made quite an impression on him."

"They really got along. They went skeet shooting, and Nicholas let Daddy beat him."

Katherine laughed. "No one *lets* your daddy do anything. You know better than that!"

"Do you think Senior will give us his blessing?"

"Did Nicholas ask you to marry him, Tarah?"

"We've talked about it."

Her mother blew out a soft sigh. "Baby girl, your daddy and I only want you to be happy."

"Nicholas makes me very happy, Mama. He loves me and I love him." Her voice dropped an octave. "I've loved him since before his accident. And watching him go through his struggles and seeing the kind of fight he has in him, I only love him more."

"Then we will love him, too!" Katherine said.

Tarah grinned, her joy filtering through the phone line. "I have to go, Mama. I have a patient I need to check on."

"Give Nicholas our regards. I'm going to come visit next month, I think. Kamaya has some conference in San Diego, so I plan to go with her. We'll stop in Los Angeles to check on Guy and Dahlia, and then we'll come to see you. But you and I will talk again before then."

"Thanks, Mama! I love you," Tarah concluded.

"I love you, too, baby, and I'm very excited for you."

After disconnecting the call, Tarah dropped her cell phone back into the pocket of her white lab coat. She checked a patient's chart one last time before signing off on the request for an increase in his pain medication.

She was only slightly surprised to find Dr. Harper standing behind her when she turned, the man staring at her intently. Dr. Harper had become an unwanted fungus, showing up in the most unlikely places to wreak havoc on her comfort levels. His behavior was just shy of harassment. Despite her efforts to keep things as professional between them as she could, he seemed to garner great joy from pushing her buttons and crossing the boundary lines. She was just a signature away from filing a formal complaint with human resources and potentially ending her own career at Phoenix Hope.

She took a deep breath, forcing the hint of a smile onto her face. "Dr. Harper. I didn't see you standing there."

"Dr. Boudreaux." His gaze shifted from her face, down the length of her body and back again. It was as if he were stripping her naked with his eyes.

Tarah crossed her arms, the gesture obvious.

He smiled. "How is our patient?" he asked as he took a step closer to her.

"Our patient?" Tarah took a step back.

"Mr. Stallion. How is he doing?"

Tarah nodded. "Nicholas is doing exceptionally well. Thank you for asking."

"I saw that he has an appointment with us this week. He'll see me and Dr. Charles. There's nothing to be concerned about, I hope?"

Tarah gave him a look, annoyance furrowing her brow. "He's fine. I know his appointment with you is just a regular follow-up."

"And the urologist? Is that a regular follow-up, as well? Or is he having some...problems?" The man leered at her.

"He's fine."

"You can never be too sure in situations like this."

"We're sure," Tarah snapped. "Nicholas is well, but we appreciate your concern."

Dr. Harper took another step closer, narrowing the space between them. He leaned toward her, his voice dropping to a low whisper. "Well, I'm here if you need me," he said.

"We won't," Tarah quipped.

Dr. Harper quickly turned on the heels of his leather shoes and moved in the opposite direction. Once he was out of sight, rounding the corner to another hallway, Tarah exhaled the breath she'd been holding.

She stole a quick glance to the watch on her wrist. Harper had unnerved her, his presence always making her feel squirrely. Despite her best efforts, it was becoming harder and harder to hide her growing dislike for the man. She'd once held him in high esteem, but the respect she had for him when she'd arrived as a first-year resident no longer existed. She found him mean-spirited, manipulative, condescending and controlling. Her rejection had been a bitter pill for him to swallow, and he'd been making her pay for it ever since. He had berated her in front of patients, criticized her skills to colleagues and just been an overall ass whenever he thought he had an audience. But she'd refused to allow his personal feelings about her to impact her goals. She'd become a formidable challenge, holding her own against him in the operating room and not biting her tongue when she knew she was right.

She suddenly needed to vent her frustration and knew Dana would understand her vexation. They'd become a support group of sorts, holding each other up after the doctor's frequent childish tantrums. With the exception of her friend, Tarah had kept the verbal and emotional abuse to herself, handling it by her lonesome. She didn't dare tell Nicholas and get him riled up. He still needed the doctor's professional skills. Despite the man constantly irritating her, Dr. Harper was on point with his patients and his teachings.

Tarah reached for the phone on the desk and dialed down to the other nursing station. Dana answered on the first ring.

"Please say you have time for lunch," Tarah quipped.

"I can meet you in the cafeteria in five minutes," Dana answered. "And boy, do I have some gossip for you!"

Tarah passed the physical therapist leaving the home as she pulled into the driveway. The two exchanged a quick greeting, the man giving Tarah a thumbs-up about Nicholas's progress.

As she moved into the home, she found him still in the pool's heated water, floating on his back. An old jazz song was playing over the sound system. After a quick change into her own swimsuit, Tarah chose a more upbeat musical selection before she joined him outside.

Nicholas was hanging onto the side of the pool, his legs extended out behind him. His eyes skated the length of her body. She wore a little yellow print bikini that fit her lithe body like paint. His mouth dropped open, his eyes bulging with appreciation. It had to be a crime for any one woman to be that stunning, he mused, admiring the contrast between the yellow fabric and her warm, honeyed complexion.

As she moved in his direction, he realized he was holding his breath, his heart beating like thunder in his chest. He shook the fog he'd fallen into from his head, needing to find something else to focus on, so he figured he'd pick an innocent fight.

"Justin Bieber? Really?" he quipped, pretending not to be amused with her song of choice.

"I like Justin Bieber."

"Well, I was enjoying Regina Carter."

"She was playing a violin."

"Your point?"

"Justin wasn't playing a violin."

Nicholas shook his head. He bobbed down into the warm water, then lifted himself back up. "It's a jazz kind of day, Tarah."

"Don't get your knickers twisted in a knot. Your jazz is still in rotation. I just added Justin's new album to the mix." She eased into the water beside him. "I've had a Justin kind of day."

"Was it that bad, baby?"

Tarah laughed. "Why would that be bad? It could have been a really good day."

"You needed Justin. That says it all." He leaned over to kiss her lips. "By the way, you didn't have more clothes you could have put on?"

"Why, you don't like my swimsuit?"

"I love your swimsuit, but you might as well be naked."

Tarah shrugged. "That's doable."

He leaned closer to her. "There's a quiver of heat burning in my swim trunks right now. If anything pops off, we are having sex. We will recite our vows and then I'm making love to you. I'm just putting you on notice. You can blame that little bitty bikini, because you look damn good!"

She wrapped her arms around his neck and kissed him. "If anything pops off while we are here in this pool, I will not put you on hold. We'll have our wedding night right here, right now." She reached between them and lightly trailed her hand across his crotch.

Nicholas closed his eyes and chanted. "Pop off, pop off, pop off, pop off…" He opened one eye and feigned a pout. "Damn, damn, damn, damn, damn!"

Still giggling, Tarah pushed herself off the side of the pool and swam one lap to the other end. She turned and swam back, pausing once again at Nicholas's side.

"Your therapist said you had a good workout. Are you tired? Do you need help getting out of the pool?"

"Nope! And it was a great workout. But the water feels really good. I'm not ready to move back into my chair. I'm on a mission right now," he said, lifting his eyebrows suggestively.

Nodding her understanding, Tarah swam a second lap, enjoying her own time beneath the water. The tension that had tightened the muscles across her neck and back was suddenly gone. She swam back to Nicholas's side again as he watched her. When she'd finished five laps, her breathing labored from the exercise, she swam to the concrete steps that led into the pool and sat down. Nicholas was already sitting there, leaning back against the pool wall with his arms outstretched. With both his hands he lifted one leg and then the other to shift his body some, giving her more room beside him.

Tarah leaned her torso against his, allowing herself to melt easily into his arms. Nicholas wrapped his arms around her and drew her close as he pressed a kiss to her forehead. "I missed you today," he whispered softly.

She smiled. "I missed you, too."

Tarah sat with him for a good long while, the Arizona sunshine beaming down on them. The light reflected off the crisp blue water, and from where they sat, the mountains in the distance reflected off the wet surface. "That would make a beautiful painting," Tarah said as she pointed out the imagery for him.

He nodded as he looked where she stared, following the line of her index finger. "Too bad neither one of us paints," he said.

Tarah laughed. "Are you hungry?"

"I'm actually starving. I didn't eat lunch today."

"Why didn't you say something?" Tarah asked as she stood up.

Nicholas shrugged. "I knew I'd eat. Eventually. I was just enjoying this time with you."

"Let me help you get into your wheelchair," she said as she stepped out of the pool to pull his chair closer, maneuvering it to the edge of the pool.

Nicholas shook his head. "I'm good. Why don't

you go on in? Put some clothes on or something. I'll be right there."

"Are you sure? I can help…"

"I said I can do it." His tone was abrupt, and it stunned Tarah.

A wave of concern pierced her expression for a second, but she forced a smile onto her face. Taking a deep breath, she tossed him a nod of her head as she moved across the patio and stepped inside.

Standing in the doorway, Tarah watched him. An air of sadness had flooded Nicholas's face, and she found it disturbing. She wanted to rush back to his side to make him smile. He sat alone for a good few minutes, lost in thought, and as she studied him, she would have sworn that he was praying. His lips moved slightly, and tears misted his eyes.

When he finally moved, she took a step back behind the curtains, not wanting him to catch her observing him. She watched as Nicholas lifted himself onto the edge of the pool. His muscles bulged, his upper body strength extraordinary. He scooted his backside over until he sat in front of the chair, turning so that he could grab the chair's arms with his hands.

It happened in a split second, Tarah suddenly realizing her mistake. She cried out, calling his name as she rushed back through the door. But it was too late. When she'd moved the chair, she'd forgotten to lock the wheels in place. As Nicholas used all of his might to push himself up into the seat, the chair slid abruptly from beneath him, rolling off into the grass. It threw Nicholas off balance and he fell hard, hitting the concrete with a loud thud.

"It was an accident!" Nicholas said, his voice raised. "I will have accidents!"

Tears streamed down Tarah's face as the emergency room physician set his arm in a cast. She was talking to Nathaniel on speakerphone as she explained what had happened.

"It was all my fault," Tarah sobbed. "I was trying to help. Now I've set him back two steps."

Nicholas shook his head. "Tarah, it's no big deal. You act like it's the first time I've fallen. I forget to lock the wheels on my chair sometimes, too!"

"I shouldn't forget!" she cried out. "I should know better!"

"He's going to be fine, Tarah. Do you need me to come back?" Nathaniel tried to reassure her.

Nicholas yelled. "No! I'm good. I told you it was no big deal!"

The doctor shook his head. "I'm keeping you overnight for observation. That's a nasty bump on your head."

Tarah brushed the tears from her eyes. She groaned, the anxiety that swept through her consuming. "I am so sorry," she said, repeating the statement for the umpteenth time.

The doctor gestured for her attention. "I've ordered a room for him, and I placed a call to Dr. Harper and his medical team. They may want to order some additional tests."

Nicholas's gaze skated around the room. "I'm fine," he exclaimed, frustration washing over his expression.

The doctor nodded. "Better safe than sorry, Mr. Stallion."

"Tarah? Hello?" Nathaniel's voice sounded from the device in Tarah's hand. She and Nicholas looked at one another, having forgotten that his brother was still on the line. Tarah apologized.

"It's no problem, but the doctor's right, Nick. They need to check you out. Just to be safe," Nathaniel admonished him.

Nicholas closed his eyes briefly. He fell back into the pillows, pulling his good arm over his head to shade his eyes. Spending the night in the hospital was the last thing he wanted to do. He listened with one ear as his brother and his girlfriend concluded their conversation, Tarah promising to call Nathaniel if anything changed with his condition.

It took no time at all for them to transfer Nicholas to a private room. The doctor on call came to check his vitals and give the nurse on duty instructions. Once he was settled in, Tarah pulled up a chair, determined to remain by his side.

"You should go home."

"I'm not leaving you, Nicholas. You may need my help."

"Tarah, it's only a stress fracture. I don't even know why they put it in a cast. The doctor said it will be back to good in a few weeks."

"They put it in a cast to make sure you don't do any more damage."

"Whatever, but we're not talking about me. We're talking about you. You need to go home and get some rest. You've been working nonstop and you're exhausted. The last place you need to be is here in the hospital with me."

"Being with you is the only place I should be."

"And I appreciate that, but you also need to get your rest, and you can't rest well watching me all night long."

"I'm fine!"

"You're not, Tarah. You are the most levelheaded woman I have ever known. Your emotions are always in check. You don't cry, and you definitely don't cry in front of people. But you've been bawling like a baby since you called the ambulance to come get me. That tells me you're exhausted and you need to get some rest."

"I want to be here, Nicholas," she said, moving to the side of the bed to sit next to him. Tears pressed hot behind her lids again, and she blinked them back.

He touched his good hand to her cheek, his fingers caressing her gently. "And I want you to go home. Please. Do it for me."

Tarah shook her head. "Are you upset with me?" she asked, apologizing yet again. "I really didn't mean to be so careless. I am so, so sorry!"

"I'm not upset, Tarah. It wasn't your fault."

"Can't I do anything for you?" she asked. "I have to do something, Nicholas!"

He nodded. "Yeah, find me a hamburger and some fries. Then go home, get some sleep and pick me up in the morning."

Nicholas's overnight turned into a four-day hospital stay. Dr. Harper had some concerns, wanting to run a battery of tests to ensure everything was well. Relief flooded Nicholas's face as the doctor confirmed the results of his last CT scan.

"The swelling we were initially concerned with is gone. Everything looks good. How are you feeling?"

"I feel good," Nicholas said. "I'm ready to go home."

Dr. Harper nodded. "Well, I'm going to sign your release papers. It'll take a minute for them to get everything together, but you'll be home before the afternoon is over."

Nicholas extended his good hand, shaking the doctor's. "Do you by chance know where I can find Dr. Boudreaux?" he asked. There was a hint of excitement in his tone, the wealth of it shimmering in his eyes.

Dr. Harper smiled. "Tarah's in surgery at the moment. She has a full schedule today. Do you need me to pull her away?"

Nicholas shook his head. "Oh, no! I just wanted to share the news with her. I'll see her when she gets home tonight."

Dr. Harper smiled, a twisted smirk appearing. Nicholas swore he saw a hint of deception trickle across the man's face.

"I hope I'm not overstepping my bounds, but I'm glad we have a moment to talk."

Nicholas met the man's gaze. "Is something wrong, Doc?"

Dr. Harper took a seat at the end of Nicholas's bed. "I don't know if she told you or not, but Tarah and I spent quite a bit of time together before your accident. In fact, I didn't even know the two of you were in a relationship until your accident."

Nicholas nodded. "Tarah and I are very private people."

Dr. Harper hesitated. "Okay, if you say so."

"Where are you going with this, Doctor?" Annoyance pressed like a lit match against Nicholas's spirit.

"Tarah's a good friend, and I'm concerned about her."

"Excuse me?" Nicholas shifted forward slightly.

Dr. Harper paused as if he were choosing his words carefully. "Tarah has a brilliant career ahead of her. She has worked extremely hard to get to this point in her surgical career, and she's been making quite a name for herself in the field. But lately she's been distracted, and rightfully so. But a distracted surgeon makes mistakes. Tarah can't afford to make mistakes.

"Obviously it's important to her to be here to support you. I don't know how serious you two are, but I wouldn't want to see her continue to make all the sacrifices she's been making for you, then lose herself and everything she's worked so hard for if you two don't work out."

"Tarah's not going to lose herself," Nicholas said defensively.

Dr. Harper smiled. "I'm sure you don't think so, and I'm sure you don't mean to be a burden to her, but let's face facts, Mr. Stallion. Tarah has hopes and dreams that she will never see come to fruition. She once talked about having children, a family, a stellar career and a partner to share that with. She never once talked about being a caregiver."

Nicholas bit down on his bottom lip to stall the quiver of emotion that had suddenly hit him broadside. "And your point?" he finally muttered.

Dr. Harper moved back onto his feet. "Sometimes, Mr. Stallion, patients see only what they want to see. As your doctor, I would do you a great disservice if I didn't point out things you *need* to see. That, and I wouldn't be a good friend to Tarah if I ignored what I see happening to her." He moved to the door and, with one last glance over his shoulder, made his exit.

Nicholas sat in stunned silence for over an hour, the conversation replaying over and over again in his head. He couldn't deny that everything the good doctor had said had concerned him at one time or another. To have the man put it so bluntly made him think that he'd been deceiving himself, and her, to believe that what they felt for each other was enough to get them through. He pressed the call button for his nurse. When he became impatient, he used his one good hand to lower himself into the wheelchair that rested beside the bed. The effort was exhausting, and he struggled for a minute to catch his breath.

Rolling himself to the open door, he paused, catching sight of Tarah and the doctor huddled in conversation at the other end of the hallway. Dr. Harper was whispering in her ear. There was a smile on her face, and he clutched her shoulder too casually. And then the doctor kissed her cheek.

Nicholas rolled himself back into his room. He was lost in reflection again, not sure what to think about his relationship with Tarah. Moving back to his bedside, he reached for his cell phone and dialed his brother.

"Noah, hey! I need your help."

Tarah's eyes widened. She was stunned into silence. She took a big step backward, shaking herself out of Dr. Harper's grasp.

"We're very proud of you, Dr. Boudreaux," he said.

Dana looked from one to the other. "Is everything okay, Tarah?" she asked, moving to stand by her side.

"Everything is just fine," Dr. Harper answered. "I was just congratulating Tarah. Dr. Boudreaux has been named this year's recipient of the prestigious Field Foundation Award from the Society of Neurological Surgeons. The award recognizes individuals for outstanding and continuing commitment to research in neurosurgery."

"My goodness!" Dana exclaimed. "Congratulations!" She threw her arms around Tarah's shoulders and hugged her.

Dr. Harper nodded his approval. "This is one of

the greatest honors that can be given to a neurosurgeon," he said.

Tarah was still in complete awe. She hadn't even
known she was in consideration. The award recognized the accomplishments of a neurosurgeon with
exceptional surgical proficiency and an outstanding
work ethic. Her research studies and her mentoring
skills with young people pursuing academic neurosurgery careers had only added to her qualifications.
The tribute acknowledged everything Tarah believed
in, and to have her hard work culminate in such an
honor left her stunned.

"I need to go tell Nicholas!" she said, her gaze
shifting down the hallway. "He's going to be so excited for me!"

"I'm sure," Dr. Harper said. He looked at his
diamond-encrusted wristwatch. "Your good news
will have to wait, though. You have surgery."

Tarah looked down at her own watch. She'd had
only a thirty-minute window of free time between
her last surgery and her next. She'd been headed to
Nicholas's room to check on him when Dr. Harper
had cornered her. Their conversation had started off
awkwardly, Dr. Harper lauding her with praise. And
it had surprised her. For weeks he'd been ignoring
her, refusing to allow her near the operating room.
She'd been relegated to grunt work, and she had done
it with a smile on her face, refusing to let him get the
best of her. Then, out of the blue, she was scheduled
for back-to-back surgeries, barely having time to eat

or pee. The extremes, topped with Nicholas breaking his arm, had put her on emotional overload.

"You are scrubbing in, aren't you, Dr. Boudreaux?" Dr. Harper had started down the hallway toward the elevators, turning back for her attention.

Tarah gave him an anxious smile. "Yes, sir," she said reluctantly. "I'm coming."

She tossed Dana a look. "Would you tell Nicholas I'll be back up to see him as soon as we're finished? It should be about an hour, maybe two."

Dana nodded. "I'll do that right now," she said.

Tarah gave her a quick hug, then raced off, catching up with Dr. Harper, who was still lauding her with praise.

# Chapter 11

Tarah's two-hour operation took just under seven hours to complete. By the time she was able to release the patient from recovery and change into a clean pair of scrubs, the sun had set and a full moon sat high in the evening sky.

After checking all of her patients one last time, she took the elevator up to the fifth floor, anxious to see Nicholas. Bursting into the room, she was surprised to find a strange woman lying in the bed and what she guessed were her three adult children and husband visiting her. Tarah apologized profusely for the intrusion as she backed herself out of the space.

Dumbfounded, she moved down the hall to the nursing station. Just as she reached the desk, Dana called her name, seeming to appear out of nowhere.

"Hey, did you talk to Nicholas? Do you know where he is?" Tarah asked.

Dana nodded. "Dr. Harper released him."

Confusion washed over Tarah's expression. "Released him? When did that happen?"

"This morning."

"This morning? That doesn't make any sense. During surgery he was making snide comments about me wanting to check on Nicholas. He never said a thing about releasing him."

Dana grabbed her hand and pulled her down the hall. She didn't speak until they'd entered the elevator, the conveyor doors shielding them from prying eyes and ears. "Dr. Harper is a snake!"

"I don't understand. What the hell is going on?"

"I was talking to Valerie, Nicholas's nurse, and she said she overheard Dr. Harper telling Nicholas that he was being a burden to you. She said he really went in on him about holding you back from achieving all of your goals. Valerie said she thinks the conversation knocked Nicholas offside. He didn't look happy. She didn't want him to feel embarrassed that she'd overheard the conversation, so she figured she would give him a moment to himself. But when she went back to the room, he was gone."

Tarah began to shake, something like rage building. It was a fast burn, and she knew that it would take very little time before she combusted into a full-fledged firestorm. She felt Dana grab her forearm, sensing her distress.

"I called your home to check on him, but he didn't

answer," Dana said. "I'm sure he's there waiting for you."

The elevator door suddenly opened, making an unexpected stop on the second floor. Dr. Harper stood in wait, his mouth lifting in a wry smile when he saw them. Tarah suddenly felt like she was trapped in the middle of a really bad movie, everything that could go wrong playing out on the big screen.

"Ladies, good evening!" he said as he stepped into the conveyor and pushed the button for the first floor. "Are you two headed out to celebrate Dr. Boudreaux's good fortune?"

"You told Nicholas he was a burden to me?" Tarah snapped. "Who the hell gave you the right to speak on my personal relationship?"

The man's gaze narrowed as he looked from one woman to the other and back again. He cleared his throat before he spoke. "I told him the truth!" he spat. "I explained to Mr. Stallion that much is expected from a doctor of your caliber. He will never be the man you need him to be. And you don't need a man who is going to hold you back. You deserve better. So I told him what he needed to hear. What you *both* needed to hear!"

The elevator opened onto the first floor. Dr. Harper gestured for both women to exit.

Stepping out of the space and into the foyer, Tarah spun back around to face him. "Dr. Harper, make no mistake, I have truly valued my time here at Phoenix Hope. Being under your tutelage has pushed me to be a better doctor and an even better surgeon. Not only have I learned what *to* do, but I've learned what *not* to do. And what I have never done is allowed my personal life or my personal feelings to get in the way of my professional judgment."

Dr. Harper's jaw tightened. The color had drained from his face, and he looked as if he'd seen a ghost. He was grinding his teeth and his eyes narrowed, ice seeping from his stare as she continued.

"Nicholas Stallion is my personal life. And you allowed *your* personal feelings about my relationship with him to cloud your judgment. So now allow me to give you some advice. Nicholas is a better man than you will ever imagine being. He has exceeded my expectations, which is why he has my heart. He will do more with no legs than you will ever be able to accomplish. You aren't even man enough to wipe his sweat! You, sir, are pathetic and small and undeserving of my friendship *and* my respect."

"You can't speak to me like that!"

"Dr. Harper, I don't plan ever to speak to you again. Tomorrow I'll take this up with Human Resources, and I'm going to file a formal complaint about your harassment. I'll also be giving my notice. You can take this job and you can shove it right up your narrow…"

"Tarah," Dana called her name, interrupting the rant she was about to spew.

Dr. Harper bristled. He hissed through clenched teeth, "All I did was try to save you and your career. If you can't see that, then maybe you don't deserve to be here. So do whatever you think you need to do. If you really believe anyone is going to take your complaint seriously, you're fooling yourself. You have no proof that I did anything wrong!"

There was a long moment of silence as Tarah narrowed her gaze on the man's face. Her body tensed, her hands clenched into tight fists and he took an abrupt step back, something like fear pinching his expression.

A smirk crossed Tarah's face. "Don't be so sure of that, *Thaddeus*!" And then she turned, storming out the hospital's front doors.

The interior of the house was dark when Tarah pulled into the driveway. She suddenly got a sinking feeling deep in the pit of her stomach. She had tried a few times to reach Nicholas by phone, but he hadn't answered. She sat in the car for a moment, staring at the outside night-lights that illuminated the property. She was still shaking with anger and frustration, whispering a prayer for God to give her a hand.

Moving inside, she called Nicholas's name. When she got no answer, she raced from room to room searching for him. He was nowhere to be found, and when the reality of that settled over her, she felt completely lost.

She moved to the answering machine to see if he had left her a message, but there were no calls, the little red light not blinking. He hadn't called the house or her cell, and she was suddenly furious with Nicholas, even more than she was with Dr. Harper.

She dropped to the floor, her heart racing as anxiety swept through her. In her mind's eye she imagined the tongue-lashing she planned to give Nicholas when she finally saw him. She crafted each heated word and every irate nuance in her head. She had some choice names she planned to call him, the list lengthy and terse. And then she planned to wrap her arms around him, hold him tight and never let him get away from her again. She swiped the tears from her eyes as she tried to fathom where even to begin her search for him.

Her cell phone chimed in the palm of her hand. Recognizing the number, she answered on the first ring. "Nathaniel, do you know—"

"He's in Utah. Nicholas flew back home."

"But how…?

"Apparently he called Noah. He hasn't been there that long, but Naomi says he's locked himself in Noah's guest room and he's not talking to anyone. He needs you, Tarah."

"He left me!" Tarah felt her anger rising again.

"No one ever said my brother was the most logical! He's impulsive and he doesn't always think things through, but he loves you, and you love him. And right now, he desperately *needs* you."

"I don't understand why he would run off like that without talking to me. I really don't."

"He's scared and he's feeling out of control. He doesn't know how to handle that."

"Maybe, but what if he doesn't want me? Maybe this isn't supposed to work out between us."

"Do you really believe that?" Nathaniel questioned.

Silence filled the space between them as Tarah pondered his comment. She finally took a deep breath, blowing the air out heavily. "I need to call the airlines," she said. "I need to get on the next flight out."

"Just pack a bag. There's a plane waiting for you at the airport."

A Fly High Dot Com corporate jet sat on the tarmac, the flight crew preparing for takeoff. Nicholas's sister-in-law Cat Moore owned the multimillion dollar aircraft leasing company. Tarah had enjoyed meeting Noah's wife over the holidays, and as the staff went out of their way to ensure she was comfortable, Tarah was impressed.

"Ms. Boudreaux, we'll be ready to depart in about thirty minutes."

Tarah smiled up at the female pilot, a tall redhead with large eyes. "Thank you," she said. "Is it okay to use my cell phone to make a few calls?"

The woman nodded. "Of course, and if you want access to the internet, we do have Wi-Fi." She smiled brightly as she moved back to her preflight checklist.

Tarah's first call went to Nicholas's voice mail, where she left one more message for him to call her back. Her second call was to Nathaniel to let him know she had boarded the plane and would be landing about two hours later.

"I'm not sure who'll be there," Nathaniel said,

"but someone in the family will be there to pick you up."

"Does he know I'm coming?"

"No. We all think the element of surprise will work to your favor."

"You want me to ambush him?"

Nathaniel laughed. "Personally, I want you to do whatever it takes. If you need to beat him, feel free to do so!"

Tarah smiled, shaking her head from side to side. "Thank you," she said, her voice quivering slightly.

"My brother is a very lucky man," he said before disconnecting the line.

Tarah's last call was a conference call with her sisters as she filled them all in on everything that had happened.

"What are you planning to say to him once you get there?" Maitlyn asked.

"After I cuss him or before?" Tarah quipped.

Kamaya laughed. "Please don't hurt that man!" she teased.

"No, you need to hurt him!" Katrina retorted. "You need to get him straight. I can't believe he just up and left like that."

"Didn't you run away from Matthew after a misunderstanding?" Tarah questioned.

Katrina laughed. "That was different."

"No, it wasn't," Maitlyn said. "And it's a good thing Matthew went looking for you or you'd still be crying your eyes out!"

"I did not cry!" Katrina bantered back. "And this is not about me!"

"Tarah, are you sure about this? Did you ever consider that Dr. Harper might be right?" Kamaya asked.

"No," Tarah said emphatically. "I love Nicholas. And he loves me! Dr. Harper doesn't have a clue what that means or how it feels." Tarah took a deep breath before she continued. "I can't breathe without Nicholas. I feel like the bottom has fallen out of my world, and right now I'm falling into a big black hole. I need him more than he will ever need me, and I have never needed any man! He's a big piece of my heart, and right now my heart is completely broken. I never knew it was possible to hurt this much!"

"How can we support you?" Kamaya finally asked, breaking through the silence. "Because you know we'll do whatever you need us to do."

"Pray for me," Tarah whispered. "Then start planning my wedding, because I will get my man back."

Maitlyn laughed. "Do you still want to get married in a castle with a moat around it?" she asked, surely remembering back to one of Tarah's childhood dreams.

Tarah laughed with her. "I'd marry Nicholas in a tree house in the middle of the Louisiana swamps. I just want to be his wife."

"Well, we're here if you need us," Kamaya concluded, all the Boudreaux girls concurring.

"Oh, and one more thing," Tarah said before ending the call. "Katrina, I need an attorney," she said.

"I want to move forward in resolving that problem we talked about."

"What problem?" Maitlyn asked.

"Her Dr. Harper problem," Kamaya answered.

Katrina chuckled. "I'm on it, baby girl. Don't you worry. You focus on Nicholas. I'll take care of helping you keep your dream job."

Tarah smiled. "Thank you. I really love you guys!"

Nicholas could hear whispering. Then there was silence, with one or both of his siblings leaving the home. He relaxed into the quiet, grateful for the moment of peace and silence. Noah and Naomi had been mumbling under their breaths since he'd gotten off the plane. His decision to leave Phoenix had been abrupt, but in his mind, necessary. His siblings just didn't understand.

Despite what was in his heart he couldn't shake the doubt that Dr. Harper had put in his head. If he would've spoken to Tarah, he knew she would have tried to stop him, and he would have let her. It wouldn't have been fair to her, and he loved her too much to tax her with any more of his issues.

His cell phone rang once again, and he sent the call right to voice mail.

"How long are you going to ignore her?" Noah asked as he suddenly loomed large and imposing in the doorway.

Nicholas's shoulders jutted toward the ceiling. "I don't know what to say to her," he finally answered.

"Maybe you need to start the conversation with an explanation and then an apology."

Nicholas met his brother's stare. Noah moved into the room and sat down in the wingback chair across from him.

"You wouldn't understand," Nicholas said. "And I know Tarah won't understand. Hell, I can't even make sense of it."

"It doesn't seem that complicated to me," Noah said. "You faced a little competition interested in your woman, and you didn't trust that she would choose you. So you ran scared."

Nicholas tensed, his brother's comment feeling abrasive. He shook his head. "That's not… I can't…" He trailed off, desperate to find the words. "Harper was right. Tarah deserves better."

"Did Tarah ever tell you that? Did she ever make you *feel* that way?"

He shook his head. "It doesn't matter. She can do better than me. I'm damaged goods!"

Noah shook an angry finger. "You are not *damaged*, and I know for a fact that Tarah never once treated you like you were. In fact, from what I saw, and what I know, Tarah has never treated you any differently from how she treated you at the ranch during Christmas. A woman who will love you like that isn't a woman you turn your back on."

Nicholas thought about his brother's comments. He hated admitting that Noah was right. And he hated knowing that he'd made a horrible mistake.

In the distance a door slammed, and Naomi's

voice suddenly echoed from the hallway. "Noah's right. You've messed up big time! If I were Tarah I wouldn't have anything to do with you."

"I guess it's a good thing you're not Tarah," Nicholas snapped back.

His sister moved into the room, shooting Nicholas a quick look. She turned, directing her comment at Noah. "I picked up some Chinese food from Charlie Chow's after I ran my last errand. No one's had anything to eat, and I knew neither one of us wanted to cook."

"So, we're good?" Noah asked, his eyebrows raised. He and his sister exchanged a look, something secretive shifting between them.

Naomi nodded. "We are. I don't know about him, though," she said, tilting her head in Nicholas's direction.

"Leave me alone, Naomi. I really don't need you giving me a hard time right now."

"I'm not giving you a hard time, Nicholas. I'm just stating facts. You messed up and now you have to pay the piper. Isn't that how your mother used to say it?"

"Norris Jean also used to say that a hard head made for a soft ass!" Noah laughed.

Nicholas shook his head. He turned his chair so that his sister was looking at his back, his eyes shifting toward his brother. "I need to fly back to Phoenix. I need to talk to Tarah. Can I lease one of your planes, please?"

"Now he wants to talk to Tarah!" Naomi exclaimed, tossing up her hands.

Noah shook his head. "Let's all get something to eat first. Then we'll figure out your next steps."

"Did you stop to consider that Tarah might not want you back?" Naomi interjected. "If you'd bailed on me, I know I wouldn't want you back!"

Panic suddenly washed over Nicholas's expression as he considered that Naomi might be right. "I should call her," he said as he pulled his cell phone from his pocket and pushed the programmed number for Tarah. The phone rang over and over, then went to voice mail. Tarah wasn't answering his call. He didn't bother to leave a message.

He shifted his gaze toward his brother and sister, the two eyeing him with amusement.

Naomi shook her head. "You are such a man!" she exclaimed as she exited the room.

Noah laughed. "Let's go eat," he said.

Nicholas nodded. "I need to wash up," he said. "Then I'll be right there."

His brother turned to make his exit. Minutes later Nicholas was having a hard time steering himself out of the bathroom. His brother's home was not conducive to his wheelchair. Trying to maneuver his way with one good arm didn't help his situation. Frustration furrowed his brow as he struggled to back himself out of the small space.

"Do you need help?" Tarah asked, her voice sounding from the other side of the room.

Nicholas's head whipped around as he turned in his seat. "Tarah?

She stood up, slowly sauntering to where he was stuck in the doorway. "The entrance is too narrow for you to wheel yourself if you don't take it really slow.

"Move your hands out of the way," she commanded as she rested her palms on the handles, pushing him forward slightly, then pulling him backward until his chair cleared the door. She pushed him to the center of the room and stood by the chair his brother had been sitting in earlier. The two locked gazes.

"Your electric chair would have been so much better had you stopped by the house to get it before you snuck off," she said smugly.

"I was going to call," he said, his voice dropping to a loud whisper.

"When? Later tonight, tomorrow, a year from now? When were you going to call to break up with me, Nicholas Stallion?" Her hands dropped to her waist, clutching the round of her hips. "Because that's what you were planning to do, right? Break up with me? So what is it? You've fallen out of love and you don't want to be with me anymore?"

"Tarah, you know that's not true."

"Do I?" She suddenly raised her voice. "Because you left me! You left *us*, Nicholas! You actually abandoned our relationship!"

He tossed up his good hand in frustration. His one arm in a cast made the simplest gestures awkward. "I was messed up, Tarah. I wasn't thinking. But I do love you, and I know you love me."

"But you didn't trust it. Dr. Harper fed you a line of garbage and you were suddenly ready to throw what we had away."

"I'm sorry," Nicholas said, regret wrapping him in a blanket of lament. "I'm so sorry."

Tarah crossed her arms over her chest, shaking her head. "So am I, Nicholas."

He rolled himself to her side, reaching to wrap his arm around her waist. He felt her body quiver at his touch, the heat between them rising. He pressed his face into her abdomen, inhaling her familiar aroma. "How do I make this up to you, Tarah? Because I would do anything to make this up to you!"

Tarah encircled his head and shoulders with her arms. She leaned down to kiss the top of his head. "I don't know if you can, Nicholas. I trusted you, and you should have trusted what we had."

He looked up into her face. "So, what now?"

Tarah kissed him one last time, then stepped out of his embrace. "If you want back in this relationship with me, Nicholas, you're going to have to work for it. And I don't plan to make it easy on you," she said. She headed toward the room's door. "I'll make arrangements for your brother to get your stuff out of my house."

Nicholas looked stunned. "You don't want me to come back to Phoenix?"

Tarah stood staring at him for a moment. "No," she said finally. "You don't deserve me."

# Chapter 12

Nicholas pushed his Chinese food around on his plate, the sesame chicken and fried rice tasting like dust. He had no appetite, his want for food barely registering on anyone's radar.

Tarah had disappeared from the family home as quickly and as quietly as she'd appeared. He had tried to chase after her, but maneuvering his wheelchair around his brother's furniture and the stairs and not being able to run had made that impossible.

His family had been of no help, his siblings sitting down to enjoy their meal as if nothing had happened. Both had actually found something funny about the whole situation.

"Did she have a taxi waiting for her or what?" Nicholas asked, shifting his gaze to his brother.

Noah swallowed his bite of orange beef and swiped his lips with a paper napkin. "No, she borrowed my car. She'll leave it at the airport, and Naomi will run me over to get it in the morning."

"She flew in on one of your planes?"

Noah nodded. "Yes. Just like you did. Two hours from door to door."

"I'd forgotten how pretty she is," Naomi interjected. "Tarah is so pretty!"

"She is beautiful," Noah agreed.

Nicholas looked from one to the other. "You two think this is funny, don't you?"

"I don't," Noah said as he took another bite of his food.

"I think it's funny as hell!" Naomi laughed. "I can't wait to call Natalie and catch her up!"

Nicholas cut an evil eye at his sister. He turned back to Noah. "Why did you help her leave?"

"I didn't. Her brother Mason chartered her return flight. She has surgery tomorrow or something like that. Whatever it was, she insisted she needed to get back home tonight."

Nicholas pushed himself from the table.

"Where are you going?" Naomi asked. "You didn't eat. You have to eat to keep your strength up!"

"I need to figure out how this went so far left and try to make it right."

His sister fanned a hand at him. "That's easy. I really don't know why you men make things so difficult."

"What do I need to do?"

"Exactly what you did to win her heart in the first place. Whatever it was that captured her attention from jump."

Nicholas pondered the suggestion. He lifted his eyes back to his sister. "And if that doesn't work?"

Noah laughed. "Then you're going to need to figure out how to handle seeing her with another man at our family gatherings."

Tarah slept soundly on her return flight. She knew Nicholas was safe, and that knowledge brought her immense comfort. So even though she was still heated with him, rest came easily. The trip there and back had allowed her to think long and hard about Nicholas and their relationship.

Being with him had been an abundance of firsts for her. He'd been the first to break down her reservations, allowing her to trust that she could be vulnerable with a man and it would be okay. He'd been the first man she'd ever said *I love you* to. With Nicholas she had always seen what they could do together, never focusing on what he couldn't do because of his disability. And she had trusted him. Like she trusted her father and her brothers. Confident that he would protect her and not hurt her heart. And he was the first man she had ever gone chasing after.

Her chasing of Nicholas was why she had told him that coming back would not be easy. He would have to want her as much as she wanted him if they were ever going to find their way back to each other. He didn't deserve her making that easy for him.

It was past midnight when she finally arrived back at her home. After locking the door behind herself, she engaged the alarm system and headed straight for her bed. When the quiet became too much to bear, she turned on the sound system, flooding the house with music. Nicholas's soft jazz painted the walls with a hint of melancholy. She suddenly missed him more than she'd ever imagined. She missed his smell, his laugh, the sound of his snore when he slept well at night. And she missed his touch, his hands hot and teasing as he held her when they slept, sometimes stealing a pinch when she least expected it. How much she missed his Stallion touch. Tarah allowed herself to cry, her tears hot as they rained down the curve of her cheeks.

One week after leaving Phoenix, Nicholas began to call Tarah faithfully, his daily messages so numerous and consistent that Tarah could have set her clock by them. She smiled as she pushed the play button on the answering machine.

"Tarah, hey, it's me. I just wanted to tell you that I was thinking about you and I miss you. Are you ever going to call a brother back? Sometime soon, maybe? Okay, then. I love you, baby. I just want to know that you're well."

Her smile widened as she pushed the save button, adding the message to all the others he'd left. After that long week of silence, Nicholas called and kept calling but Tarah had yet to pick up or return one of his phone calls.

Kamaya cut an eye at her sister as she passed Tarah a cup of coffee. "How long do you plan to make him suffer?" she asked.

Tarah shrugged, a smile lighting her face. "Trust me," she said, "Nicholas isn't suffering that much!"

Kamaya laughed. "We were all wondering if you saw those pictures."

Tarah took a quick sip of her brew. "Everyone saw them," she said, referring to the tabloid photos of Nicholas and that actress from a popular prime-time ABC television show. The leading lady had been posed in his lap, one leg thrown out high, her head tossed back as she squealed with delight. It had been a good shot. The image had come from his first endorsement photo shoot since his accident. Nicholas had left twelve messages to explain it away, desperate for her to know that the leading lady hadn't meant anything to him.

Katherine set two plates of shrimp and grits in front of her daughters. "You young people play too many games. You better call that boy back before he gets tired of calling."

Tarah laughed. "He won't get tired. Nicholas Stallion loves me."

Her mother shook her head. "Then it's past time you *let* him. He's learned his lesson. You're not doing anything now but torturing him."

Tarah met the look her mother was giving her. "It's not about torturing him. Nicholas needed time to himself. There was a moment, just before he fractured his arm, when I realized he was struggling.

All the time we'd been spending together since his accident was great, but it hadn't given him a chance to redefine who he was as a man. He still had to discover what it would mean for him no longer to be an athlete or never to walk again. He needed to learn that his masculinity isn't exclusively located below his waist. He had issues to resolve in his head, and he couldn't do that while we were so busy trying to define who we were as a couple. I realized I had to let him go in order for him to come back and be the man I needed him to be."

She took another deep breath, holding it briefly before letting it go. "That and I needed to get past being angry with him. Because it really hurt my heart that he left the way he did without talking to me. We can't do this if we don't talk. Good and bad. We have to be open and honest with each other. If we'd returned to the way it was, with everything going on with me at the hospital and him feeling inadequate, we might not have made it. Now I think we have a fighting chance."

"Even with his challenges?" Kamaya asked.

"I know that whatever his future needs may be, I won't be able to fulfill them all, and I shouldn't try. We may need help, and neither one of us needs to be afraid to ask for that help. But I love him, and it scares me to think of what my life would be like *without* Nicholas more than it does to imagine being with him."

Her mother nodded. "You never cease to amaze me, Tarah!"

"Me, too!" Kamaya chimed. "Damn, that was deep!"

"What have I told you about cussing?" Katherine admonished her, swatting a hand at her.

The sisters both laughed heartily. They continued talking until the doorbell interrupted them.

"Are you expecting someone?" Katherine asked.

Tarah shook her head. "No, ma'am."

"I'll get it!" Kamaya shouted as she jumped to her feet and rushed to the foyer. She returned minutes later, a large bouquet of mixed orange and red freesia arranged in the prettiest vase. "Someone got flowers!" she chanted.

Katherine shook her head, chuckling warmly. "Bless his heart!"

Tarah leaned in to sniff the sweet aroma wafting off the stems. She pulled the card from the envelope and began to read, the assembly of words moving her to laugh until she had to swipe a tear from her eyes. "I told you he loves me," she said.

Kamaya snatched the card from her sister's hand, reading the message aloud. "'Tarah, are you ever going to cut me some slack? It's hard picking flowers for my girl from my wheelchair. My wheels keep running over the plants! Love, Nicholas.'"

Katherine moved to Tarah's side, wrapping her arms around her shoulders. "Don't you ignore that boy anymore!"

Nicholas dropped his phone against the marble counter of the center island in his kitchen. It had been a long day and he was exhausted, wanting a shower and his bed. He'd had therapy that morning, working with his team of trainers. After that he'd grabbed lunch with his brother and then had gone on to play a game of wheelchair basketball with some new friends he'd made at the rehabilitation center. They'd played hard, and he was now feeling like he'd been run over by a train.

He'd called Tarah. She still hadn't answered or returned his calls, but he took that as a good sign. He knew her well enough to understand that if she was done with him, she would have sent a message for him to stop calling altogether. There would have been no doubt about her not wanting to hear from him ever again.

Instead their siblings were having a grand time keeping them updated on each other. He knew Nathaniel kept her abreast of his progress, reporting what his new team of doctors had to say about his health. And he was certain that the one time he'd gone to dinner with his buddy after her Wimbledon win, both his sisters had rushed to share the details. He had left messages about everything else.

He'd been excited to tell her that he'd reconnected with some old college friends who were doing a great job holding him down and giving him a hand when he needed it. He'd given her a blow-by-blow of his decision to return to his penthouse apartment in Los Angeles, investing in the renovations to make it wheelchair-accessible. He'd become self-reliant and independent, loving that his paralysis was more of a footnote than the entire essay of his life experiences.

Thanks to her brothers, he knew that Tarah had filed a sexual harassment lawsuit against Dr. Harper. His cousin Matthew had kept him updated, passing on the news that they expected him and the hospital to settle quietly in Tarah's favor. Dr. Harper had since accepted a teaching position abroad, not at all missed by the fifteen women who had joined Tarah in her complaint against him.

Earlier that day he'd learned that she had officially completed her surgical fellowship. She'd passed her board certification exams and had earned her unrestricted medical license. She was also being honored for her achievements in a formal ceremony taking place some weeks to come. Even with the distance between them, they had family rooting for them, and they were always rooting for each other.

An hour later, when Nicholas was settled in watching the ball game on his big screen television, the video chat line on his computer rang. His excitement was suddenly combustible as he pushed the remote to answer it. Tarah's shining face filled the oversize display.

"Hey!" he said, joy gleaming from his eyes.

"Hey, yourself," Tara said, smiling sweetly.

"How are you?"

"It's a good day," she answered. "Can't you hear Justin playing?"

Nicholas laughed. "I see your taste in music hasn't improved since I've been gone."

Tarah laughed with him. "Maybe not, but I'd be

willing to bet that you're still watching reality television when you think no one is looking."

He grinned. "Some things never change."

"And some things do," she said. There was a moment of pause as Tarah allowed the reflections to billow between them. "Thank you for the flowers. I wanted you to know how much I appreciated them. They're beautiful." She slid the vase into the camera's view so that he could see them.

"I miss you, Tarah," Nicholas said softly. "I miss the hell out of you!"

Tarah's smile blossomed like the flower buds beside her, the upward curl of her lips lifting slowly. "Can I call you later?" she asked, promises gleaming from her stare.

Nicholas nodded. "If you don't, I will call you."

In no time at all they were back on track, sharing time and space within the confines of their digital world. Tarah's schedule was still chaotic and his wasn't much better. The time they were able to video chat or talk on the phone became important to them both.

When Nicholas answered the early evening call, he was surprised to see Tarah and her friend Dana holding two babies, a third woman beaming in the background.

"Hi," he said, confusion washing over his expression.

Dana tossed up her hand, smiling as if she'd swallowed a Cheshire cat.

"Hey! I had some special visitors today and I wanted you to say hello. They're going to be big fans one day. Nicholas Stallion, this is Oscar and this is Henry Barton. They had to come in for their checkup today, and their mother asked about you."

The woman behind Tarah waved excitedly. "My husband and I are big fans!" she exclaimed.

Nicholas laughed. "It's a pleasure to meet you, Mrs. Barton. And your boys are beautiful!"

Tarah smiled. "These two munchkins are tough, and they're doing exceptionally well." She pressed a warm kiss to little Oscar's cheek before passing him back to his mother. The two women and the babies stepped out of the camera's view.

"You look good with a baby in your arms, Tarah!" Nicholas said, his eyebrows raised.

Tarah giggled. "Hush your mouth, Nicholas Stallion. What have I told you about cussing at me?"

"I didn't cuss!"

"No, you tried to put a curse on me. That's even worse!"

"I did no such thing. I just made an observation."

Tarah grinned. "I just wanted to say hello. I'm on duty, so I need to run. I've got surgery in an hour."

He nodded. "I understand. Will we talk later?"

Tarah nodded. "Definitely. I was thinking about coming to see you. We can talk about it tonight, but I have some time off soon, and, well…maybe I can come visit?"

"Was that you inviting yourself, Tarah Boudreaux?"

Tarah smirked. "Not at all, but if you want to extend an invitation, I might be open to accepting it."

Nicholas smiled. "Call me later and we'll talk about it. I'll need to see if I have any openings in my schedule."

Tarah laughed. "You know you can't wait to see me!"

Tarah woke him from a sound sleep when she was finally available to call. He grappled with his phone, the device falling out of his hands twice before he could finally pull it to his ear.

"Hey," he whispered, before realizing he'd talked into the earpiece and it needed to be turned around. "Hello?"

Tarah chuckled softly. "I didn't mean to wake you. Go back to sleep."

"No, I was waiting to talk to you. I wanted to hear your voice."

"You were sound asleep."

"I still wanted to hear your voice so I could dream about you when I go back to sleep."

"You flatter me, Nicholas Stallion."

"Then I've done my job successfully!" he said, a smile filling his face. "How was your day?"

"We've been slammed. There was a nasty accident on the interstate, and we've had a lot of traumas come through. It's been a busy day."

"Sounds like you need some sleep yourself."

"And I'm ready for it, too. But I had to call and talk dirty to you first."

"Brilliant and freaky! You're a dream come true!"

"I try to please!"

Nicholas stretched his arms up and out, the phone clutched between his shoulder and his ear. He struggled to suppress a yawn. "Baby, I can't keep my eyes open, but I really need to talk to you," he muttered.

"I understand," Tarah replied. "Is everything okay?"

"I'm not going to be able to fly in for your awards thing next week. I forgot that I had promotional gig that I'm committed to."

"Oh…okay," Tarah said, disappointment paramount in her tone. "I was really hoping you'd be there."

"I was, too, but you know how it is."

"No, I don't," she said, attitude ringing loudly in her voice. She took a deep breath and held it.

"We'll see each other soon, Tarah. Are you still thinking about flying here for your vacation? We'll see each other then."

She exhaled the air she'd been holding. "Let's talk about it in the morning," she said.

Nicholas voiced his agreement. "We have a few things to talk about," he said, then added, "We really need to make some decisions about where this is going."

"Excuse me?"

"Our relationship. I'm really not feeling the long-distance thing anymore. I can't see you being so happy about it either. Besides, even though we're back on speaking terms, I don't know that we've made a whole lot of progress. You know what I'm saying? We need to make some decisions one way or the other."

"Where's this coming from?" Tarah asked, his comment surprising her.

"Are you saying you haven't thought about it?"

Tarah hesitated. "I really hadn't…"

Nicholas interrupted her. "Well, give it some thought. It might be time for us both to move on. But we can talk tomorrow. Sweet dreams, Tarah."

"Good night," Tarah said, but Nicholas disconnected the call before she could get the words out.

Tarah sat in a slight stupor for a moment, replaying the conversation over again in her head. She was suddenly feeling all out of sorts. She'd thought they were back on the right path, traveling on the same route, but somewhere along the way it seemed Nicholas had turned off in another direction. Maybe her mother been right and she'd taken too long to lead him back to her.

In his own bed, Nicholas fluffed the pillows behind his back and head. He tossed his phone to the other side of the bed and closed his eyes. As sleep slid in to reclaim him, a slight smile played on his mouth, amusement pulling him toward his dreams. He'd heard the disquiet rising in her voice. He could just imagine what she was thinking. And he couldn't wait to kiss every ounce of her anxiety away.

# Chapter 13

From the pout on her face, no one would have known that a milestone moment in Tarah's young life was about to occur. She found everything annoying, her temperament was surly and she felt like she would spit bullets if someone looked at her wrong. And all because her feelings were hurt.

She had spoken to Nicholas only once during the week and very briefly. He had blown her off for something he claimed he just had to do. They had played phone tag for all the other calls, continually missing each other. They still hadn't had a conversation to address his last comments about the two of them going in separate directions.

Now here she was, surrounded by the people she loved most as she was about to be honored. And

Nicholas wasn't there with her. Even Noah and Nathaniel and both their sisters were there to show their support. Nicholas was doing some photo shoot for a men's cologne. He thought that was more important. She suddenly found herself wondering if this was the beginning of the end for the two of them.

"Tarah, baby, you really need to try and smile," her mother said, stepping behind her to play in her hair. "Frowning ages you, dear." The matriarch brushed a loose strand back into her updo.

Tarah turned slightly in her seat to meet her mother's gaze. "I think I messed up," she said, her voice low.

Katherine squeezed her daughter's shoulders. "What did you do, baby?"

"I think I gave Nick *too* much time to think about things. I think I'm losing him."

Her mother slid into the seat beside her. "That's just silly. Why would you think that?"

"For starters, look around. You don't see him here, do you? I would never have believed that Nicholas *wouldn't* be here to support me. He knows how important this is to me. Second, he actually told me that he wouldn't miss this for anything in the world. He *promised* he would be here! But suddenly, taking pictures with some half-naked, high-profile model is more important. It's like I'm not a priority anymore."

"Actually, it sounds like you're whining to me," Katherine attested. "Nicholas has tolerated your bad behavior for a while now. Not answering his calls, ignoring him. I have no doubts there have been times he wished you were there supporting him while he was going through a lot, and you weren't anywhere to be found."

"But I explained why I treated him the way I did."

"You did and you were right. Nicholas did need some time to work through his stuff. But sometimes how you do things could use a little work, baby girl."

Tarah drew a hand to her heart. "I really am trying to get better, Mama!"

"Well, you need to stop worrying. That boy truly cares about you. He's not going anywhere anytime soon."

"Which is why he should be here. I really wanted to see him."

"I have no doubt that if Nicholas was getting some sports award and you had to choose between that and brain surgery, you'd be in the operating room."

"Yeah, but there are no half-naked top models in the operating room."

Her mother laughed. "Sounds like you might be a little jealous."

"Damn right! Nicholas is a great catch. Other women don't need to know that. He's *my* great catch."

Katherine shook her head. "I'm going to ignore that cussing this time, but next time I will pop you in your mouth. You know this!" she admonished her.

Tarah laughed. "Yes, ma'am. I need to touch up my makeup and get to the table."

Her mother leaned in to kiss her cheek. "Good. I was starting to wonder if you were going to spend all night in this powder room!"

\* \* \*

Senior Boudreaux was holding court, giving his sons and the Stallion men a life lesson about women.

"You can only say *yes, dear,* so many times before you need to nip that quick. Be a man in your home! Your woman needs to trust that you know how to take control and be in charge. You might have to make some decisions that she isn't going to agree with, but you always have to do what you know is right for your family."

"I don't know about all that," Kendrick said. "I love her to death, but sometimes it's just easier to let Vanessa have her way than to hear her noise!"

The guys all laughed.

Mason shook his head. "You'd better listen to Senior. He wouldn't have been happily married for half his life if he wasn't on to something. I don't think there's one of us here who doesn't want what he and Mama have. I know I do!"

Tarah's brother Donovan snorted softly. "You know you let Phaedra do whatever she wants most times. And I'm not going to lie. Gianna has me wrapped around her finger, too."

"I admit I spoil my woman just like you spoil yours. There's nothing wrong with that." Mason chuckled. "And she shows me her appreciation on a regular basis," he added with a wink.

Senior shook his head. "You spoiling your sister is why poor Nicholas here has his hands full with Tarah. She's my baby girl and I love her to pieces, but she's determined to give a man a hard time!"

Nicholas laughed, the others laughing with him. He was enjoying the exchange between the men in his family and hers. The conversation was easing his nerves. Anxiety had started to bubble up as he thought about the surprise planned for Tarah. He finally responded. "Tarah is definitely a challenge, sir!"

"You don't have to tell me, son! And I'm sure Mason is secretly thanking you. He won't have to sneak and help pay his sister's bills anymore!"

Mason laughed. "No, I'm thanking him out loud! I'm not ashamed to admit that I've never been able to say no to *any* of the girls. Now we just have to find a man for Kamaya and I'm good!"

Kendrick laughed. "Until Phaedra gives you a daughter. Then you're really in for it!"

Senior chuckled in agreement.

The men had all been standing in a circle around Nicholas. It had taken some maneuvering to sneak him into the banquet venue for the awards program and keep him from the prying eyes of Tarah and her sisters. He'd come to surprise her, and all of the Boudreaux and Stallion males had lent him a hand.

It had also been his opportunity to speak with her father and brothers at the same time, pleading his case for her hand in marriage. He knew that when he asked Tarah to marry him, he would need their blessings. He was thankful that each and every one of them had excitedly proffered his support.

One of the event planners gestured for their attention, waving them to their seats. "Gentlemen, the program will be starting in about five minutes. Mr. Stallion, we need to get you to the presenters' side of the stage. It will be easier for you to maneuver your wheelchair from there."

Nicholas nodded. "Thank you. If you can give me one minute, please."

The woman smiled. "Just let me know when you're ready," she said as she moved off to the side, giving instructions to the lighting guy and the woman responsible for the trophies.

"Are you going to be okay?" Nathaniel asked his twin.

Nicholas took a deep breath and nodded again. "I think so. I'm nervous, but I'd be worried if I wasn't."

His brother extended his arm, and the two punched fists before Nathaniel turned, following behind the others.

Senior let his sons and family move ahead, leaving him and Nicholas alone for a moment. He dropped a heavy hand on Nicholas's broad shoulder, tapping him affectionately. "I'm very proud of you, Nicholas. You didn't let your injury stop you from continuing to achieve your goals. And you haven't allowed my baby girl to run all over you."

"No, sir. I've had to rethink what those goals will be, but your daughter has been my inspiration. I love Tarah. I know I come with some challenges, but I promise you, sir, I will do whatever it takes to make her happy."

"I have no worries, son. Tarah won't let you do any less than that!" Senior said with a deep chuckle.

"Congratulations! Now I need to get to my seat so I can hold my wife up when she finds out I knew something before she did!" He tapped Nicholas one more time before he headed off in the opposite direction.

Nicholas was grateful for the moment alone to collect his thoughts. He shifted in his wheelchair, adjusting his tuxedo jacket and ensuring his iron-creased slacks were straight. He wanted to make sure he was polished to perfection when Tarah laid her eyes on him for the first time.

He closed his eyes, his hands clasped together as if in prayer as he reflected back on everything that had gotten him here. Pieces of a puzzle falling easily into place.

Tarah had been excited to tell him about Kyle Barksdale, the former linebacker and sportscaster turned humanitarian journalist, who had been selected to host the prestigious medical event. She was a fan of the man's writing and was looking forward to the opportunity to meet and talk with him. Nicholas hadn't bothered to tell her that he and Kyle were old friends, both having roots in Salt Lake City. And that's when the idea had come to him. He planned to use this moment to show Tarah and the world just how deep his level of commitment to her was.

One phone call to his agent, another to Kyle who called the awards committee, and six degrees of separation later, Nicholas was the celebrity face who would be honoring the nation's most promising neurosurgeon for her dedication and work in the field. He would also be asking the magnificent doctor to be his wife, to make their alliance official. He took a deep breath and then a second.

His thoughts were interrupted as his friend Kyle appeared at his side, and he reached out to shake his hand, his arm no longer in a cast.

"It's good to see you," Kyle said as he leaned down to give his old friend a hug.

"It's good to see you, too! It's been a long time."

"Too long. We both need to do better."

Nicholas nodded. "I appreciate you reaching out after my accident. I didn't do a very good job of showing my appreciation, but I had a lot going on."

"Hey, man, it's all good! How are you doing now?"

Nicholas grinned. "I'm still making that paper! I just signed a new endorsement deal with Tag Heuer, and I'm in negotiations with Gatorade. I'm also the new face of Fly High Dot Com!

Kyle laughed. "I ran into your brother Noah. I hear you had an inside lead on that one!"

Nicholas laughed with him. "I'm not going to lie. There was a little nepotism involved, but I had to beg hard to get the gig! Noah's wife is a hard sell when it comes to her business."

"I met your girl," Kyle said, changing the subject. "If I wasn't already married, I might have to give you a little run for your money. Beautiful, intelligent and she likes my writing! You chose well!"

Nicholas grinned. "Man, she picked *me*! I'm just one lucky son of a gun!"

"Well, congratulations. I'm happy for you, bro!"

"Thanks, man. I really appreciate that!"

The event planner gestured for the two of them.

"You ready to get this show on the road?" Kyle asked.

Nicholas reached into the breast pocket of his jacket, his fingers brushing against the velvet ring box secured inside. "Yeah!" he said, his face beaming with joy. "I've been ready!"

Tarah was twisting her hands nervously in her lap. There was a ton of long-winded speeches, and she was ready to be finished and back home in her bed. She'd tried to reach Nicholas twice, wanting just to hear his voice. But her calls had gone right to voice mail, and she wasn't sure what to make of his disinterest. She sighed, a gust of warm breath blowing past her glossed lips. She felt her mother trail a hand across her back, and she lifted her eyes to the matriarch. Both of her parents were beaming with pride.

"Ohh! This is it!" Kamaya exclaimed.

"We're so proud of you!" Maitlyn chimed.

Tarah turned her attention back to Kyle, who stood on stage at the podium.

"Thank you, Dr. Raeford. And now for the event of the evening! I am honored to introduce our next guest, who will be presenting the Field Foundation Award to this year's recipient. My esteemed colleague is renowned for his exploits on the football field. He was an All-American and a Heisman Award winner and was ranked one of the nation's top-rated passers. We all cheered, and cried, as he took his current team to their last championship victory, which resulted in a traumatic injury that has left him confined to a wheelchair. But nothing is keeping this good man down. I learned while speaking with him recently that he owes his recovery to the skills and dedication of a neurological surgical team that included tonight's award recipient. Please, put your hands together and help me welcome my friend, quarterback extraordinaire, Nicholas Stallion!"

As Nicholas wheeled himself out onto the stage, Tarah felt the hairs on the back of her neck rise and curl. Heat flushed her face, and it took everything she had not to begin to bawl. Her family was clapping enthusiastically beside her, and everyone in the room was on their feet to celebrate him.

He moved to Kyle's side, and his buddy shook his hand, hugged him a second time and passed him the microphone. He took a step toward the back of the stage as Nicholas rolled himself in front of the wooden pedestal. There was a moment of pause as the applause continued, and then everyone retook their seats. Tarah sat at the edge of her chair, still trying to figure out what he was doing there and why she hadn't suspected anything.

"Thank you. Thank you very much," Nicholas said as he gestured for everyone's attention. His deep voice was commanding as it resonated over the sound system. "I am honored tonight to present this year's Field Foundation Award." Nicholas went on to explain the award's history and the importance of it in the medical industry. He then read Tarah's bio, extolling the accomplishments that had earned her the honor. And then he called her name. "It is my privilege to introduce you to this year's award winner, Dr. Tarah Boudreaux!"

Tarah's legs felt like rubber as she stood up. Maneuvering her way up the short flight of stairs to the stage, her whole body shook. Nicholas was grinning in her direction. The moment she reached his side and he grabbed her hand, her tears fell, clouding her view.

Nicholas entwined his fingers between hers and pulled her hand to his lips, kissing the back of it. Tarah wrapped an arm around his neck as she leaned to press her mouth to his in a deep kiss. In that moment, she slid back into the familiarity and comfort of him, every ounce of anxiety dissipating. He gestured for her to take the microphone. When she did, reciting the acceptance speech she'd rehearsed in front of her bedroom mirror, she could see out of the corner of her eye that his chest was bursting with pride.

After Tarah thanked all of her family, his family, her instructors and the doctors who'd nurtured and supported her, Kyle stepped forward, reclaiming the mic. She turned as if to exit the stage when the man stopped her in her tracks.

"Dr. Boudreaux, I'm sorry, but before you go back

to your table, we have one more presentation. If Dr. Boudreaux's family would please join us on stage?"

Tarah looked confused as her eyes flitted back and forth curiously. Nicholas was still staring at her intently when her people and his encircled the two of them. Kyle passed the microphone back to Nicholas, then eased out of the way.

Tarah's anxiety suddenly came back with a vengeance. She hugged her crystal trophy to her chest, clutching it so tightly that her fingers began to throb. She turned her gaze back to Nicholas, and the two locked eyes.

His voice was like buttered cognac, smooth and easy, each word reverberating between the two of them. "Ladies and gentlemen," he started, "if you'll bear with me for a moment, I'd like to tell you a short story.

"During this last championship game my life changed exponentially. It was losing the use of my legs that showed me what I was truly made of, and it demonstrated the power of our hearts and souls when there is love in our lives. This extraordinary woman and I were just beginning to know each other when my accident occurred. And whereas many women would have run from the situation, the woman I was in love with hunkered down for the long haul. There hasn't been a day since then that Dr. Boudreaux hasn't shown me her support and her love. As I arrived at the hospital, she told me that she had my back, and she wasn't kidding. Now I need her to know that I have hers and that she will always be able to depend on me."

Nicholas took a deep breath. "Tarah, under normal circumstances I would get down on one knee to do this," he said, eliciting a few nervous chuckles from the crowd. "But since that's obviously not an option for me…" He paused, tossing a quick glance over his shoulder. When he did, all the men in their two families dropped down to one knee for him.

Tarah clasped her hand over her mouth, her tears burning hot behind her lids a second time.

"Tarah Boudreaux, I love you. You are everything to me. I am a better man because of you. I triumph because you are cheering me on. We are formidable together, and I know that God put you in my life for a reason. I never want to lose you again. So, would you honor me by becoming my wife? Will you marry me?" He lifted the lid of the black velvet box, exposing a brilliant solitaire diamond in a simple platinum setting.

With her tears falling, Tarah nodded her head. "Yes, yes, yes, yes, yes!" she exclaimed as she threw her arms around his neck.

As Nicholas pulled her down into his lap, kissing her earnestly, their families erupted in cheers, and the entire room gave another standing ovation.

# Chapter 14

Just days later, with their family looking on, Tarah and Nicholas exchanged marriage vows down at the Gila County Clerk's office, the justice of the peace presiding over their ceremony.

Nicholas had been the only one who'd not been surprised to hear that Tarah wanted to forgo a lengthy engagement and a lavish ceremony. After hours of nonstop conversation, the two were of the same accord, both wanting to be legally married on paper, already pledged to each other in their hearts.

She wore a short white lace dress that featured illusion sleeves and a sultry V-back. It was simple and elegant. Nicholas donned a navy blue suit, not bothering with a necktie. The joy Nicholas and Tarah exuded was stupendous, the entire family swimming in the abundance of love.

When the license was signed and sealed, they celebrated back at their new home, Nicholas surprising Tarah with the title to the Pleasant Valley property. Unbeknownst to her, he had purchased the house from her brother, since Tarah loved the life they lived there. The hospital had offered her a permanent position on their surgical team, and neither felt a need to change a thing.

Their reception was an impromptu pool party with some Texas-style barbecue and Louisiana gumbo. A good time was had by all.

"He's flying back to Los Angeles tomorrow," Tarah said, sitting in Nicholas's lap, his arms wrapped tightly around her.

"What kind of honeymoon is that?" her sisters questioned.

Nicholas laughed. "Not the one we want, but one that's necessary for the moment."

Tarah nodded. "Nicholas has a doctor's appointment at the end of the week that he can't miss, but I've got to get back to the hospital."

"What are you two planning to do?" Kamaya asked. "Is this going to be some kind of commuter marriage? You in one state and you in another?"

"Not at all," Nicholas interjected. "I'll be back by the weekend. It shouldn't take too long for me to reestablish my medical care here. I will have to travel to handle some of my business until I find office space here, but we'll make it work. Arizona is going to be our home."

Tarah kissed him, her mouth skating gently over his. As she pulled away, her gaze danced with his. "We plan to raise our babies here," she said softly.

Hours later, the house was finally empty. Their sisters had cleaned away the remnants of the celebration, returning it to mint condition. Nicholas was bare-chested, wearing only a pair of gray cotton sleeping pants. Tarah lay cradled beside him in a black lace tank top and matching boy shorts. Her thick curls were pulled into a loose bun, a few strands framing her face. Nicholas drew his hand down the length of her bare arm, marveling at just how blessed he was.

Tarah linked her fingers into his, the rising heat between them teasing. "Isn't there something you want to ask me?" she said softly as she placed a damp kiss into the center of his palm.

Nicholas smiled, light shimmering in his eyes. He gestured for her to lean in closer as he whispered softly into her ear. "There is," he said as he trailed his tongue across the line of her earlobe. "Can I touch you, Dr. Stallion?"

Tarah pulled his hand to her mouth and slid his index finger into the warmth. She suckled it gently. Nicholas gasped loudly, heated sensations sweeping through him. She stared into his eyes as she pulled away, falling headfirst into the pure, unadulterated lust that steeled his gaze. "It's *Mrs*. Stallion to you," she said. Then she slowly repeated the gesture with each of his remaining fingers.

Nicholas nuzzled his face into her neck, tracing a line of soft kisses against her skin. "I'll take that as a yes," he said, and then he did.

* * * * *

*He's got all the right moves*

# Places in my Heart

# SHERYL LISTER

Omar Drummond has closed himself off from emotional entanglements. With Morgan Gray, it's different—he craves more. But proving herself as a sports agent means securing the football superstar as a client, not a lover. To win her, he'll have to show her that he's playing for keeps.

## THE GRAYS *of* LOS ANGELES

*Available October 2016!*

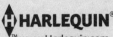

KPSL470